Restoring PATTERNS

GABRIELLE F. CULMER

iUniverse®

RESTORING PATTERNS

This is a work of fiction. All of the characters, names, incidents, organizations, and dialogue in this novel are either the products of the author's imagination or are used fictitiously.

iUniverse books may be ordered through booksellers or by contacting:

iUniverse
1663 Liberty Drive
Bloomington, IN 47403
www.iuniverse.com
1-800-Authors (1-800-288-4677)

ISBN: 978-1-4917-9017-5 (sc)
ISBN: 978-1-4917-9018-2 (e)

Library of Congress Control Number: 2016903039

Print information available on the last page.

iUniverse rev. date: 02/29/2016

Contents

Chapter 1

DAY OF HEARTS

Kascey, an assistant designer, had a full task: it was fashion week, and she was in the city of bright lights. The designer studio was near Bryant Park; it was close enough, and she could feel the excitement of the day pulsating through her.

Vasquez Lake was the head of the corporation; it was his line and his ideas. She repeated his creations for him, and it was remarkable how creative he was. He was already at the show with sixteen models in his camp, and the fast pace and energy electrified the stage with his couture.

Kascey was only a few moments away, and she was carrying the orders for lunch—if anyone would have any. *Where is the office assistant on days like today? Obviously doing other chores*, she thought hastily.

Moda, the new face of the winter season, was on their team; the women had become closer after many days of preparation. It began with a fabric puncture, and then trust had been established.

This season, it was all red, white, cream, and black. Everything was full of basic tones, asymmetrical, and almost retro to the eighties. That decade was vaguely in her memory; now at the bright age of thirty-two, but it was a fabulous time for Vasquez.

Vasquez was extremely talented and a native of the city. The industry was all that he knew. He trained at the top design school in the city and in the fashion district in Paris. He contained the knowledge which anyone would yearn: which fabrics were appropriate, the linings, and the contours. It was his entire world. Kascey had worked for him for five years and was exposed to the cutting edge of the industry. The studio was appropriately based on the outskirts of the Garment District; the bargain hunters looking for fabric, buttons, and beading were enchanting to the youthful apprentice's eye and the source of all fashion creativity.

Kascey had fashion and style in her constitution. She was the daughter of a former town seamstress and dressmaker, Mabel Kann, who started her own manufacturing and retail-clothing factory. Mabel had learned how to stitch at an early age by using the most difficult of fabrics and the most sophisticated styles of stitching. Kascey benefitted from this background; she was elegant, narrow, and tiny in stature so that the clothes hung off her as if she was a model who had been raised in Paris or Milan. This week they have New York, next week they have London, and the following week they have Paris Fashion Week; their travel plans were entirely organized. She trotted in her stilettos to the show, overloaded with bags for the group and everything they had forgotten.

Vasquez trusted her with his world; he saw her as talented, reliable, and serious about the craft. She was his protégé. Her beige, Fifth Avenue–bought coat swayed as her elegant black dress slightly emerged from underneath as she walked. She was trained in the old school with knowledge of fashion, which came naturally and from being raised in the industry. Her history of seamstresses and couturiers in her background dated back to the flapper era when a few would sew for aristocrats or socialites in some far off international jurisdiction. It was a world far from hers now and her abode in Greenwich Village.

She was stuck at the crossway at Thirty-Eighth and Sixth and was almost there. Finally, she approached the entrance to the venue, showed her pass, and waltzed in confidently as if she did it every day. In fact, one could say that she basically did, and this was no exception. However, she was essentially late.

"Ah, Kascey, you are here," Vasquez said. "Fabulous. I am famished. Thanks for bringing this on your way, I am on a special diet. Set that down over here. I will let Mari handle it. Get the dresses from the racks and start assigning them for the show. I want the beige and red for Moda. Moda, please come over here. Kascey, please pass this to her," ordered Vasquez relieved to see her.

Kascey looked over to see Moda in the front of the stylist having her face made up for the show. Moda looked in Kascey's direction with a still palette of a face. Kascey had seen the blank look before and understood that Moda Riche had already transformed herself into her model character. "Here, this is for Moda," she said as she passed the veggie wrap to Mari.

"Thanks," Moda murmured, hardly able to move. Her hair was halfway twisted up with the other half bone straight. Moda was from France and extremely experienced. She was also at least six inches taller than Kascey at a towering five foot eleven inches.

Moda was famished and could not wait to savor some chocolate from her valentine, which was on her mantelpiece at her apartment in Chelsea. She managed to devour a few bites of the wrap. It was already half an hour until the next segment, and she just needed enough nourishment to concentrate. Now ready for her part, the red and beige ensemble draped her stately figure as she scrunched her feet into her black heels and practiced her movements. *Sometimes it has to hurt to look good*, she thought as they were evidently a size too small. Her practice was not necessary, but it was habitual for her. It made her unique and professional at the same time; she got into gear mentally and physically at the admiration of others.

Vasquez was on cloud nine from the hype of the show as he greeted the other designers and models who shared the room. It was the first of the shows, and they would have repeat sessions in Europe over the coming weeks.

Kascey immediately continued concentrating on the selection with Vasquez. She had her mending kit ready in case something would tear. Kascey was all booked and was confident that her significant other understood from past years. He was a stockbroker who lived downtown. New housing had developed, and he had a bright penthouse apartment overlooking the Hudson, with gaping windows. He was dedicated to his trade and mixed the success of his field with the glamorous life of Kascey.

* * *

To Grady J. L. Chisholm, she was an eye-catcher, and they attended the best galas and charity events in the city. He hardly needed home-cooked meals, and often they ate at the newest restaurants from the Flatiron District to Downtown Manhattan. He envisioned a fashionable life for his fashion expert and wanted to see her evolve to the making of her own designs. After all, she had the expertise and the background. With her credentials and his funding, she could make it anywhere. He felt that it was his job to make her even more popular in her field. His dreams were as far and as vast for her as his eyes could see from his corner office with views of the southern part of the city.

"I know that you have your own course in life you wish to take," he had said to her. "However, I can help you guarantee that it will be a reality."

He recalled her perplexed look as if he had just overstepped his boundaries. At the time, she hardly knew him and he understood her reaction. After that conversation, he knew she was the right person for him.

This year he would make the journey to Paris for the weekend after the show because the two needed a winter break. He hoped to propose by the holidays because they had been together for three years, but he did not think she would be ready to slow down her life. She kept a book of her own sketches that she had been working on since design school. He knew that "Kascey Couture" could be a success. He had flipped through the pages on one of the first evenings that he visited her apartment and was highly mesmerized by her sketches.

"These are really impressive," he said. "Are you planning on having your own design house someday?"

She nodded enthusiastically, but she was still shy around him. She had come across many established men in her time, but none who were so concerned about her future.

His parents, Damian and Kelly, lived in Maine. They owned a house in the South of France, and he had spent a few years working in Zurich after college. There had been other relationships; however, Kascey Kann was the one with whom he was meant to be. He met her in New York at a downtown fashion event that his sister dragged him to attend. Lucinda was a buyer for Marley's NYC.

Kascey was overly ambitious and serious, and she had a purpose to her step. He knew they would make it. He had not seen her type of drive, and it reminded him of his own family who had arrived a few generations ago. He saw their aspirations and a slight naiveté in her eyes, and he wanted to be there for her. Kascey had medium-brown hair and green eyes which could match most outfits. Her hair would lighten in the sun and showed a few red streaks, but it could darken for a severe, modern look with mousse. She was from Canada and had been in New York for some time. From the conversation, he remembered her rhetoric and her love of Europe, and how her grandparents, who were in retail, had moved from London to Canada to start their own manufacturing company. She bragged about the fashion in New York and her visits to Bimini, and he was flattered that someone so traveled wanted to impress him. After all, Toronto was not far from where he was raised in Maine.

He had spent summers on the Cape while she had spent her summers in Bimini and the Keys. Eventually, Grady attended an exclusive boarding school in Vermont and attended university in New Haven where he studied finance. It was through family connections that he secured a job at an investment bank in the city, which sent him on secondment to Zurich after graduation.

For Kascey, life was just as interesting. After design school, Kascey spent stints in London and in Paris perfecting her craft at fashion houses, which helped her to land the job with Vasquez whom she met at a show in Paris. She headed to New York and started a fascinating and adventurous life. It was during that period that she met Grady. To her, it was still felt like yesterday, and she felt on the top of her game when she saw him saunter in with a petite blonde who she mistook for his girlfriend.

She felt as if she had spent half the evening speaking in a way she had never spoken to anyone. He listened and was impressed, but she was more impressed by him and his lifestyle. She knew that she had met her match. He was a precise and steely character who offered to take her to his favorite French café in Paris the next time they were both there. Grady was thirty-two at the time, and she could not believe how presumptuous he was. It took her back to her life in Europe, and she felt a deep connection to him.

Meanwhile, Grady had made expensive plans for the evening that were light and fun. He knew that Kascey would be under a lot of pressure for the next several weeks as always. He thought that a quaint and close meal at Chez Louis would suffice at nine o'clock.

Looking forward to the evening, Kascey was hungry from the long ordeal over the day, and had images of the show still in her mind. She watched Vasquez walk down the runway and bow with Moda by his side. Afterward, they counted and categorized the inventory before taking all the items back to the studio. She sat with him as they went over the next day's inventory, and they had numerous counting and assembling for the casual display.

Still, she knew that she would keep this appointment, and was more than relieved to see that Grady had arrived at the restaurant and was silently waiting for her at the dinner table. As the maître d' escorted her to his table, she was overwhelmed by how packed it was. When she saw him smile and look up at her, she knew that it was a special night and that she had to cast the hectic day aside.

"Grady, I am so happy to see you. Happy Valentine's day," she said leaning towards him to greet him properly.

"Thank you. And the same to you, dear. Happy Valentine's Day," he responded.

"Have you been waiting long? I am so sorry if you have." She continued always concerned about the feelings of others before her own.

"No, not at all. I just got here myself. We had a long day at the office with the new IPO, but I really would like to hear about your day."

"Oh, it was phenomenal—as it is every year. I live for this. This is what it means to be a designer—or a mini designer as myself," she responded with a bit of humility.

"The collection this year is fabulous, and I know that it will do well once it gets to the stores. You should see the amazing dresses, and of course, Moda was superb. It was one of the best shows."

New York was Kascey's favorite location for the show since it was her hometown and she did not have to work out of hotels and other branches, but out of their studio. She could then reflect on the day in her own apartment.

He listened intently as she rambled on about the show and was so inspired by her ambition. "Really, it all sounds like fun," he encouraged her, in full anticipation of his surprise to her, that he would visit Paris with her in a few weeks, and that they would have a lovely weekend after the show. He held off and placed a small, red box on the table.

Kascey looked at it very excitedly and exclaimed, "Oh, dear, it's not—"

"Ah, no, not yet," he teased, knowing that she was not quite ready. He would wait a few more months for a more serious note.

"Aw, thanks so much. Shall I open it now?" She asked timidly as she grasped the box with her long fingers.

"Sure, when you would like," he responded fully knowing that she had absolutely no restraint when it came to gifts.

She tore open the packet and was mesmerized by what was inside.

The people at the next table thought that it would be an engagement ring and looked over inquisitively.

However, Kascey marveled at the pink, heart-shaped diamond pendant which lay in the box.

"It is so beautiful. It is magnificent and so gorgeous." She looked up at him and her eyes sparkled from his thoughtfulness. "Thank you. It means so much to me." She meant all that she said. It really did as he had been her foundation for the last three years, and she knew he was her firmest supporter. He wanted her to be all that she could be—and if that meant encouraging her to branch out into her own, then he would ensure that she did.

"I am glad that you like it. Actually, I figured you would since you have such exquisite taste." He was certain that it would appeal to her. It had cost him an arm and a leg, however, if he wanted her in his life forever, the investment had to start.

She let it rest on her fingers and watched it dazzle beneath the chandelier lighting in the restaurant. "Oh my, look at it." She was truly captivated and knew the perfect outfit with which to wear it. She glanced at him, "I have bought you something," she murmured as she took out a small box from her yellow oversized slouch bag and passed it to him.

Kascey had gotten his family crest monogrammed on a set of cufflinks. Grady wore French cuffs almost every day. She wanted to give him something special which embodied him and his family crest was the solution, as he was so interested in his ancestral history.

"Thank you, dear. You did not have to," he said obligingly. "I am sure glad that you did though." He was one for gifting and loved to give as well as to receive. It meant loyalty from someone to receive a gift in his view.

"Of course. I really wanted to. It is not as nice as what I have from you, but I hope that you will like it." Kascey had been concealing the surprise for months. She had found a small shop in Toronto that made them and was so grateful when they were able to reproduce the crest.

Grady was cautious as he opened it, and smiled as he viewed its contents.

"How did you manage to do this? It is amazing, absolutely amazing. Where did you get these?"

"Oh, I came across a shop last summer when I saw my parents in Toronto and thought of you... Really?' She responded endearingly, "Do you really like them? I think that they are perfect for you." She did not have to convince him. He truly appreciated the gift—even more so because it would someday be her family crest. It was just the type of thoughtfulness that he needed to ensure that she really was the one.

"It is so thoughtful. Thanks. I cannot wait to show them off at the office, also, my parents will love them." His parents really approved of her. It was due to her work ethic and the thoughtful things that she did that no one else would really think about.

"Shall we order? What would you like? There is a set menu or the à la carte option."

"Oh my, let's see what they have?" Kascey studied the menu and smiled at the fancy little treats that had been conjured up for the special occasion. "It all sounds delicious. This is such a good choice of restaurant. I'll have meringue and raspberry puree for dessert and the wild duck and cranberry salsa for the main course. It looks so heavenly." Thirty minutes had passed already just over the gifting, and it had to be an early night for them unfortunately.

He was pleased that she liked the menu, and he was convinced that life would be easy with her. He wished he had proposed that evening, but would wait. "Oh, I have another surprise," he said bemused.

"What? Another surprise, well dear, what is it?" At this point she was overjoyed and full of anticipation.

"Since you will be in Paris for the show in about two weeks, I thought we could have a small weekend holiday. Perhaps we can go to that special restaurant that I keep telling you about— and then who knows."

"Are you serious? That is an amazing idea, and it would be so relieving to know that you would be there after all my hard work has been completed. Thanks. I would really like that." It was true she really would. She had spent a few years there as a young seamstress and then as a designer. She had learned most of her craft there. It would be an honor to saunter through the city's streets with him and show him how she had started out. She could not wait. She had so much to do in preparation for the shows.

The couple delighted over their meal and chatted and laughed while they enjoyed the time together. They gazed into each other's eyes and tenderly reached toward each other as they discussed their trip. It was one of the most memorable evenings, and Kascey really wanted the moment to last forever.

Chapter 2
A STYLE FOR ALL SEASONS

Vasquez lived in the suburb of Westchester. He was just far enough to keep his sanity from the hustle and bustle of the city, and close enough to get there on time to design his creations.

He looked across the plush space of his garden, full of frostbite on that chilly February morning. He sipped his Italian coffee as the children rummaged through their belongings. His wife of seven years hastily prepared little snacks for their lunches. She was born on Long Island, and the family split their time between the Hamptons and the country home.

Vasquez was reputable in his community as a philanthropist and designer. He provided support to South American children's charities as a way of paying back for his success. It was important to him as he remembered the children in the vicinity of where his family originated, and he wanted to help them so that they would have aspirations of their own and become as successful as him. He was distracted and thinking about the next few weeks now that the show in New York was finishing.

"Dear, are you having breakfast with that coffee—or will you get something in the city?" She asked as she did every morning.

"I will get something later. Do not worry about me, darling, just concentrate on getting the children ready for school," he replied so appreciatively. She reminded him of his mother from Argentina. Jose and Miguel were five and six years of age respectively. They were still at the age where they were concerned about early-learning portfolios, iPad apps, and electronic games. All of which almost hung out their bright backpacks. Vasquez counted his blessings each morning because he was gracious for the stroke of luck when he started his business many years ago.

She said, "That's fine, dear. Just make sure to get something. You have a long day ahead of you.

I wish that I could make it." Daphne was still very much in love with her husband, and her idea of a special Valentine's Day was a home-cooked meal, lots of bubbly, and cards made by the children. She balanced him from all the travels and his glamorous world. They met when she was interning at a fashion house in Manhattan. She was just out of college, and she never looked back.

Vasquez kissed his family good-bye, left his coffee mug near the dishwasher, and picked up his briefcase. "Be good and have fun at school." It was the last thing that he said to the children before leaving on the frigid morning. It was already 7. 30 and he wanted to get to the fashion house by eight o'clock to gather more items for the show. It was not a particularly hectic day as the day before, but still one in which there was so much at stake.

* * *

Moda, Kascey, and Mari were already at the building collecting and gathering the dresses for the day. It was an evening theme, and Vasquez had designed his delicate black lace and pastel pink couture gowns for the next season. The final choice was Vasquez's and Moda was waiting for his vote on which to wear. Just then he strutted in full of force for the new day.

"Good morning, all. How did you spend your evenings? Very well, I hope because we have a tough day again." He warned as he greeted each of them. "By the way, fabulous work yesterday. Let's hope we can replicate it today."

"Morning, Vasquez." Kascey was still in a brilliant mood from the night before and was sporting her new pendant.

Vasquez moved in closer to view her pendant.

"Ah, let me see. Nice, nice, unusual," he said cavalierly." He turned to joke with the others. "Any more spoils from the feast?"

The group burst out in laughter and hurried back to the gowns as there was little time before they would be on again at the show. The models would be arriving soon. "Chop, chop, ladies. Let's go," encouraged Vasquez.

Moda chimed in, "You know, Vasquez, I really like the pink chiffon gown. Do you think I can wear it?"

"For you? The black lace! Why be a kitten when you can be the tiger as my leading lady? Here, this is for you." He passed her the gown which was the main piece of the collection and, which he hoped would be in households for many years to come.

"Oh, thank you," Moda replied. She wanted to tame her image this once to something more soft. "I will wear it well," she promised.

Moda had arrived in New York from Italy at about the same time as Kascey. She and Kascey had met through Vasquez. Her boyfriend, Remy, was a photographer from Staten Island and they met in the industry. His studio walls had photos of her shoots. A true New Yorker inspired by the beauty of the city and its structures. His cutting-edge photography was abundant in the tristate area. Remy was creative and had decorated his studio in roses and silk streamers. They were red and white for Valentine's Day. He had ordered a quiet dinner from their neighbourhood Italian restaurant to eat on the terrace of his SoHo loft. Her favorites were the penne with sun-dried tomatoes and Tiramisu; he was mindful of her important day ahead, and anticipated not to be splurging.

"Great. Now, let us get to it. I know that you can do it." Vasquez was optimistic and was certain that the day would turn out well again at the show. It was the precursor to London and then Paris in a few weeks, and soon the spring would blossom, and so would the creations on the most fashionable streets in the world. He was confident with his sidekick, Kascey, and did not know how he could do it again without her. The best designers of the industry were left standing and coping after the economic downturn. There was a way of holding things up. The floodgates would open again soon, and the industry would be bursting with competition.

The show flowed with elegant designs and sweeping materials as the models sauntered and strutted down the runway. Onlookers admired Vasquez's designs as Moda wrapped up the exhibit with her unique style. Afterward, Vasquez strolled out and clasped her hand. They walked with the other models to the end of the runway where he bowed. He was exhilarated by the explosive reaction of the crowd. The fashion houses of Paris and Milan awaited his arrival.

Kascey was more relieved that the hard work had paid off and that they were to embark on the fall season's preparations. She had to switch gears to the idea of heavier and deeper fabrics for the collection. She enjoyed the dainty spring materials and colors of the present collection. Now that it was over, it all set in. She felt guilty about neglecting Grady after such a beautiful evening. She checked her phone and found a sweet thank-you text 90 minutes old with no response.

"Oh no!" she gasped. She hurriedly pressed the digits in the dim lighting. Mouthing, "Sorry, did not get this, I had a l-o-v-e-l-y time, thank you," as she typed. Relieved, she felt as if she had averted disaster. *Poor Grady*, she thought.

Grady had a slightly different outlook on life. Most of Grady's life was cut and dry. He was raised with a silver spoon and yet, he had a good work ethic. Perhaps, it was mostly to compete with his peers, and when they fell out of the game, new competitors had to be found.

Kascey loved what she did. It ran through her veins. If it did not work out for her, there was always the factory in Toronto and online ordering of her fashions. She could still have a semblance of a fashion life. However, it was not the time or the place to think about that as the models filed in backstage.

As soon as Vasquez saw her, he hugged her. "Thank you, once again Kascey. I could not have done it without you."

"You are welcome. It was my pleasure as usual. What a fantastic show." She was always flattering to him. He admired her grace and certainly under pressure.

"We have to get back to the studio. We have lots more to do." He was right, there was so much more to do after the show, and so much to count and itemize. She was used to the routine and could now do it blindfolded.

"Okay, let's get it going," she responded and gestured to the staff to wrap it up.

They left with their bundles of clothing and items for the studio as cars and taxis pulled up to carry the clothing. Moda was ecstatic from the event, still reeling on cloud nine from the reaction of the crowds, and the exquisite black outfit still hung loosely along her sleek frame. She kept Vasquez and Kascey company on the way down.

Vasquez was under the stress of the industry and hoped that it would all subside eventually; he knew that the days of extravagance were gone. The cars rolled up to the Garment District, the loft, and the studio. The massive studio took up the whole floor; fabrics were draped everywhere, and items had to be put away after being abandoned in the rush.

"Ladies, I have the perfect idea for the next fall collection. You will see the Edwardian look with the bold patterns. It will be made from dark wools and plaid. However, colored pearls will brighten it up, possibly lavender and fitted waists. String up boots, oh, it will be divine." Vasquez always had a brush of inspiration in the moment of exhilaration after a show.

"Sounds fantastic," Kascey said. "I can see it all now, gray and lavender, but netting over the beanies and hats right?"

"Perfect. I knew you would have the idea. Let's order in and get to work."

Chapter 3

DOWNTOWN

Grady had a beautiful evening but had been given mixed signals, and was in the middle of the IPO. His day was different. Kascey had been the first thing on his mind, but once he got to the office, there were hundreds of e-mails and prospectus reviews. He could feel the stress surging. He had forgotten the time and was afraid to look at his watch. When he did, it was already eight o'clock. His eyes raised and he checked his phone again, nothing.

She must be pretty busy tonight, he thought. *But she has to eat.* He texted: "Must eat—will you arrive soon?" *That should do it, she has to be hungry.*

She replied, "I am really tired. It has been a long day, and I just got to the Village. Please understand. Tomorrow, lunch, I promise."

"Fine, I understand," he responded.

Texting was her way of communicating, this time to her advantage when she just did not want to discuss something. How often did she get these shows? Only several times a year, and she needed him to understand.

On that note, he switched off the computer and turned off the lights in his office. He could see the river, the lights of the boats channeling over it, and the fascinating energy of the town. It was alive, and people were out living, while he was stuck in the office, staring at the lights and then off home.

The streets were busy, as he left the building for his neighbourhood fifteen minutes away. He hopped into a cab and went on his way. It sped off to his apartment building and he paid and hopped out. His doorman was waiting and greeted him as he stepped into the elevator and glided to the twelfth floor. Again, the apartment was illuminated by the city's lights as he walked to the open and modern kitchen and opened the fridge. *Not much,* he thought and truly there was not much. *Sushi?* He clicked open a cool drink and sat on the settee in front of his computer. He enjoyed the natural light from the full moon and tried to call her on Skype, but there was no answer. *Where in the world is she?* He thought. *Oh, too bad,* and he ordered his favorite rolls.

Kascey had fallen asleep after she left the studio at about eight o'clock. She woke up in front of the TV programs still on at about 11 p.m. Exasperated she thought, *Oh no, what time is it?* She struggled as she thought that it was the next day already and she had missed work. She was still in her clothes from earlier and lifted herself to the dressing room to get ready for bed. Her West Village prewar walkup was stylishly furnished with white wicker furniture like a summer home on the Cape. It had blue and white striped carpets and shell ornaments on the wicker cabinets. She kept a beautiful photograph of her parents from one of their summer trips to Bimini. She longed for happy summer days with the smell of barbecue and baked goods while she sauntered along the shoreline, collecting shells in floppy hats and summer dresses. Her life had changed so much since then; she had never predicted herself wrapped up in city life. She stumbled into bed draped with a silk awning and covered in white, beige and sea blue cushions and linens, and fell asleep immediately.

By the next morning, the sun had arisen over a blistery cold day. She rose, peered through her window, and it had started to snow. A storm was brewing. It was perfect for the end of the week, and she had lunch plans with Grady. *Oh no,* she thought as she reached for her iPhone and saw that he had contacted her, the last time at 10:45. She checked her alarm clock and it was already 7.15. *He must be furious,* she thought as she dialed his cell.

"Good morning. I just got your messages. I am so sorry. I fell asleep. It was such a tough day yesterday, and I am relieved that it is over. Sorry."

An apology was all he needed to get over the neglect he had suffered over the past thirty-six hours. "Don't worry. I just needed to know that you were all right—and not stuck in a ditch somewhere. I am glad to hear from you. Listen, are we still on for lunch? We can meet somewhere near the Flatiron District?"

"Sure, that would be fabulous," she responded as she felt the guilty pangs from her ignorance.

She peered into his wide eyes beguilingly. "What time?"

"I think, at about one or so. I will confirm it later because I have a meeting first thing this morning, but see you soon."

"Okay, see you soon—and please forgive me," she pleaded one last time.

"Not to worry. I understand." He truly did understand. On many nights, he just dozed off and woke up in front of a TV show he had not seen in years. He now had some solace to his worries that she was fine. Did he really believe that she would just fall asleep like that though? What if it was not the case? He could not bear to think that. He took it at face value that it would all work out in the end. He just needed to think of the right time to propose.

He prepared what he would wear. He put on a navy blue wool suit, a pink-and-blue striped tie, and a crisp white shirt. *This should do the trick,* he thought. He was more concerned about seeing Kascey than about his meeting. The $200 million-IPO was routine in his world. His concept of money was that it was not an issue until it hit a certain limit and none was too high. However, he knew the value of Kascey—and she was a once-in-a-lifetime opportunity.

Kascey arose and stretched her ligaments, which had been inactive for almost ten hours. She could not believe how she had winged the previous evening and had to put on a special Friday outfit for lunch, which would also be warm enough for the weekend blizzard and then hopefully an earlier evening. She chose her cashmere camel wrap dress, black wool stockings, pumps, and a raspberry beanie to keep her head warm. It was a day for her long down coat, which was bulky, but she had to wear it.

Getting to work was a breeze. The traffic was low considering the weather forecast. The fashion district was abuzz and reeling from the show. In the fashion house, Mari was diligently working at the front desk. Corrine was steaming dresses to put on the rack.

Vasquez had not arrived and would remain in Westchester and would Skype them while Kascey and Mari prepared the pieces for the Paris show. He wanted different pieces for the show and Kascey was finishing the stitching on the evening dresses. She had ten or so and wanted the models to do a fitting ahead of the show the following week. Looking at her chores, she almost felt guilty about lunch, but had to do it.

By mid-morning, the snow had increased rapidly, but it was still clear enough to wander out in for a few more hours. She was already famished, and her fingers grew stiff as she polished the collection pieces. There were dresses draped across the working tables as she maneuvered her way around them. The ladies worked diligently until lunch when she had to excuse herself.

"I am off now," Kascey said. "I have to meet Grady. If you need to reach me, please call my cell."

"Sure. Will do. Have a lovely time," Mari replied. She was conscientiously on the computer catching up on correspondence and acknowledging orders for the new collection.

Kascey flung her warm coat over her shoulders as she headed for the elevator. "Ciao!" She exclaimed before leaving and relieved that it was easy enough. Once outside in the frigid conditions, she hailed a cab to take her a few blocks down to Pinelli's, their favorite Italian place.

* * *

Grady had arrived after his meeting and sat in a cozy seat near the corner of the restaurant. He peered through the window as the snow fell to watch for her taxi. The restaurant had checkered white and red tablecloths, wooden floors, and authentic Old World ambience. His meeting went well, and he was on the brink of issuing the shares. On Monday, it would all fall into place, and the fruit of his labor would be realized. His sister was celebrating her birthday at the end of the month, and he hoped to plan a celebration for her as soon as they returned from Paris.

Kascey swept into the restaurant a few moments late and looked around hurriedly until her glance met his. He sat patiently where she could view him at their favorite table.

"Hello, darling. Have you been waiting long? She asked apologetically.

"Not at all. I just wanted to get a good seat."

"Great. This is a good seat," she agreed, looking around to see if the waiter was nearby with the menus. She let her scarf slip over her chair. "We had a splendid morning, as you know, we are preparing for the show next week, and we are showing a different line of clothing than this week. I am so sorry you could not make it to the show. I missed you," she convinced him.

"Oh, well, you know that we had this offering, and it was just a hectic week, but I will make it up to you at the fashion show next week. You'll see," he persuaded her. He was looking forward to the break with her and had planned a lovely weekend in and around her work.

"Yes, of course, I cannot wait. I mean it will be fabulous. You will get to see all the crew again, and we can walk down memory lane. I will let you see my old stomping grounds."

"That would be splendid. I just hope that nothing crops up at work, at least with any clients over there." He had a feeling that something was brewing and work minded as he was. He figured that this would be an opportune moment just in case something would crop up at work.

"I am sure that it will be okay. You can just see them while I am at the show, you will see. It will be fabulous, and of course, we have to go to my favorite restaurant, during our brief trip." She suggested slyly and craving the wonderful crème brûlée."

"Can I get you anything to drink?" the waiter interrupted.

"Sure, please, "I'll have some seltzer water and he will…" she continued.

"Ah, just a cranberry juice for me," he added not wanting anything else to drink so soon before the afternoon meeting.

The waiter complied and handed them the menus.

"I think that I already know what I want," she said. "The salad looks good, and so does the grilled sole. What do you think?" She added only wanting to hear his opinion which would be favorable.

"That sounds great, and for me, as usual, I'll have the shrimp scampi and vermicelli. I have had a long morning—and who knows how late I will work this evening?"

"So what are your plans this evening?

"I think we will be there for quite a while, and tomorrow will be the same. I will be free on Sunday—if we are not snowed under by then."

"That is right, there is meant to be a blizzard… well I will be working whether or not we will be snowed indoors." He could envision vacant streets and staying inside the apartment.

"Oh, so sorry to hear that, as for me, I think that my hands are going to be sore before it is all over, but I will be rest assured there will be a lovely break for us."

The waiter brought the drinks, and they lifted their glass to cheer to Friday.

"Cheers," he said as he smiled at her and touched her glass with his.

"Cheers, and thank you for being so understanding."

"That is fine. It is—and always will be—my pleasure." He meant it, and she knew it, there was nothing that could get in the way of them and nothing that could get in between them.

Lunch drew to a close over espresso to continue the rest of the day. They sipped the last few drops before concluding the lunch. He walked her to the door and hailed a taxi to take her to midtown, while he headed downtown.

* * *

"Bye, dear. I will call you tonight when I am off," she promised.

"Sure thing. Talk to you soon." He slammed her taxi door.

To her, it was no longer a chore to see him. It had become natural, and she needed to help him to realize it, except, after the show as they have three in Europe fast approaching. Then spring would be theirs to share in New York.

* * *

Back at the loft, the ladies had completed lunch and were conscientious again with their fabrics. They were expecting a three o'clock call from Vasquez and wanted to give him an update. The loft grew darker as the sky thickened and the clouds deepened in the afternoon sun. It appeared as if the snow had subsided, but by the morning the worst was yet to come.

The ladies completed each design and placed the designs in the vault to secure it for the show and for any last minute detailing which Vasquez requested. It was customary for there to be dozens of dresses there, and the special dress to be worn by Moda was no exception. It had to be placed in the vault away from conniving eyes and ears. Vasquez was exceptionally protective of his gowns, and Kascey knew the procedure better than the rest through experience.

Chapter 4

CONTINENTAL PASS

The following week was hectic for the couple. Grady was reeling from the success of the IPO and he celebrated the following Friday with colleagues.

Kascey put the finishing touches on the collection for the show in Paris. She packed red, black and beige ensembles for the event. Many were packed and taken with the first group who went over the weekend; however, some were to be taken by hand with her and Vasquez on their flight to Paris. It was a trip that she had made many times before. Moda had travelled with the first group to get some proper rest before the show and would be meeting a set of models from Berlin while in Paris.

Grady would be leaving later in the afternoon. He would meet her in the morning after his flight landed and he had checked into his hotel suite. He had planned a few meetings with an auxiliary office and clients, and had to break the news to her. There still was much time for the show and he would have been free most of Monday.

The clock went off at five on Saturday morning. Her bags were packed, and there was a long checklist on the coffee table of necessities before leaving, as she would be gone for over a week because there were the London and Milan shows to follow. Her neighbor Nathalie would be checking in from time to time for any emergencies, which was a real gift to her year after year. Kascey wore comfortable black slacks, a silk blouse, and a cashmere cardigan. The group always flew business class mostly due to the amount of pieces they took with them. She had a set of Moda's dresses, in particular, for the finale in Paris. Not even she had seen the final version, and she was due for a fitting in the morning, because they did not get to the hotel until about ten o' clock local time. She remembered the routine well year after year.

Kascey emerged from her brownstone walkup with baggage in tow and walked to the car which was waiting to take her to the airport.

"Good morning, miss. How are you this morning?" he inquired as he opened the door and lifted the baggage.

"Very well. Thank you," she murmured succinctly as it was still too early to speak at that time of the day.

"That's good. Let me help you with these— and we will be on our way." He took the hint that she was not much into pleasant conversation and they drove to the airport arriving on time and within moments of Vasquez. He was struggling with the carts as the chauffer took the baggage.

Kascey signed a slip which was presented to her before her driver pulled off. She then pushed the trolley to the entrance.

Vasquez spotter her: "Good morning. How are you? Do you have everything? It is very important that we have everything," he said concerned.

"Oh, good morning to you. "Yes, it is all here. I checked it all last night, and I counted again this morning. What a disaster that would be, wouldn't it?" she expressed anxiously.

"Let's not think about that," he commented as he continued to push the trolley. "Look, Mari is already at the kiosk. Let's drop it off at the counter."

The staff were pleasant to them as they dropped their bags, mainly because they were such frequent fliers who abided by the rules. Vasquez was relieved to have that all over, however, his travel insurance was so high for the shows. They sat in the business lounge until the flight was ready to leave at eight thirty. Kascey was rather relaxed, mostly because she was organized. She checked her iPhone for the hotel's address, her credit card accounts, and her messages to see if there were any from Moda and Grady.

"Oh, look, Moda has sent a message," she announced. "She says that they got in and that she met up with Talia at the hotel, and they are waiting for our arrival."

"Great. Remind her about the fitting in the morning, Kascey," ordered Vasquez. "I hope that she will be on time, as we have so many more to fit."

"Sure, I will send her the message right now." Kascey was determined that nothing would go wrong. She managed to send a quick note to Grady who was preparing to fly that evening: *Am at the airport waiting for the flight and will see you soon, LOL, Kas.* There, now she felt better, the trip would be a dream come true.

The airline announced the flight as they gathered their belongings and had boarding passes and passports out to board the flight. Once settled on the plane, they put the dresses in the front so that they would not crease. They sipped their drinks while the remainder of the passengers boarded. Kascey felt a cringe of excitement while she envisioned her long list of chores and yearned for Grady's arrival.

The flight crew passed out refreshments after takeoff. Vasquez nestled in his chair for some quiet shut eye, and Mari took out a magazine and started to peruse the pages. They slept until it was time to get up and have a basic workday in the cabin.

Kascey was accustomed to Vasquez's way; he was so driven and ambitious. He would be uneasy until all of the dresses were back in his possession. They were worth at least $100,000. Moda's allocated dress was meant to fetch $15,000, and he still considered himself to be a middle-of-the-line specialized designer. He had learned the sophistication of the business. His New York exposure and training prepared him for the advanced minds of the experienced competitors. His smart tactics had him there at every turn to counter any problems which may arise.

The flight was not as long as expected, it felt rather short from New York to Paris. When they touched down to a Parisienne evening, the Eiffel Tower was lit in its customary welcoming tones. They gathered the dresses and bags and disembarked. It was a short walk to the carousel to pick up more belongings while Kascey checked her iPhone to confirm their arrival to the driver waiting outside. They pushed more carts and packed into the limousine which drove them to the hotel near the Champs Élysées.

Vasquez had chosen a gorgeous historic hotel where they had stayed on previous visits, and Kascey's suite overlooked the plaza and its boutiques. Vasquez was on the same floor. Grady only managed to get a regular room on a lower floor since he booked at the last minute. The city was abuzz for the show. All the hotels were booked, and models could be seen all over in anticipation of the coming days. There was glamour all over town. The city was full of talent, creativity, and power.

Kascey could not believe the detailed Renaissance furnishings and tapestries in her suite. It was like a scene out of a castle to her, but it had all the modern amenities she needed. She received a text from Grady that he was on his way. It was late in the evening with a full moon over Paris. She unpacked and turned on her favorite station to hear what the city was broadcasting over the airwaves. She found some upbeat tunes, and decided to order a meal.

She perused the menu; *let's see* the crab and avocado salad *looks good, with probably some* brie and biscuits. She settled on that and ordered it while she continued to unpack and check the dresses.

Strange. Perhaps Vasquez picked up the dress. I am pretty sure I had it when I disembarked. Oh no, she thought. *Calm down. It must be here. Look again. I don't see it. Oh No!*

She called Vasquez, who was mulling over the fashion entourage in his head.

"Hi Vasquez, do you have Moda's dress? I do not see that whole casing. Did you pick it up thinking that it is mine?" she asked timidly and cautiously.

"Let me check and call you back." He checked his bags and the closet. The dress was not there. He ran over immediately, knocked on her door to help her to look.

She opened the door frantically as he bolted in. He looked through the items, and it was not there.

"Have you checked with Mari?" He asked.

"Yes. She says that she does not have it either." Kascey was trembling at this point; one of the bags was missing.

"Call her in here —now," Vasquez said rather agitated.

Kascey picked up the phone cautiously and dialed Mari's extension and asked her to come over. She also called downstairs to see if they had anything.

Kascey was in tears. She had worked so hard on the dress and knew that it would be a hit. It was the only one of its kind and from the sketches; she would have to design a new one. If it was lost, she had to come up with a replacement similar from another pattern overnight.

The concierge confirmed that they had delivered all the bags which meant tracing the bag to the limousine company, and then checking with the airline, and the airports. She and Mari would be on the phone all night.

Moda would be meeting her in the morning thinking that she would be wearing a particular dress. Any more would not be couriered until a Tuesday arrival which would be too late. Luckily, Grady would not be arriving until the following morning, so Kascey had time to prepare and to sew.

Mari arrived frantic to the suite, and confirming that although the other delivery of clothing had arrived, the carry on was not to be found among them. The dress did not turn up anywhere. She felt absolutely helpless and despondent.

Kascey was on the phone while Vasquez looked through the merchandise to find a suitable replacement with the possibility of replicating it.

"I cannot believe it. It was the most prized piece for my star model. What are we to do? Where else can we find a red dress like that?" Vasquez was beside himself as he could not determine if anything else was missing—and now he had the headache of filing a report. He felt as though he was living a nightmare. He was concerned that something untoward may have occurred. The piece could end up on the illegal market. There were so many points of collection since New York that it was difficult to pinpoint a specific place or time. He crumbled and sat on the sofa with his head in his hands.

"Do not worry, Vasquez. I am sure that it will turn up. We must keep looking. In the meantime, we must make something else for her. I have an idea." Kascey pulled out a red dress from the ensemble, a spare, and said, "Look, I can lower the waist, widen the collar, and wrap the skirt to add pleating. We can almost reproduce it," she convinced him. However, it did not console or relieve the fact that the new design had been exposed before the show.

Kascey worked all night. Mari stood in as the fitting model until Moda arrived. They had to change the ensemble to fit the new dress because it needed to stand out from the rest. She knew that Vasquez would be pleased with the outcome— even if it were not at all how he had envisioned the collection to be presented. It would be similar with only a few minor adjustments to what the models would wear.

The sun arose over Paris on a quiet Sunday morning, it was already eight o' clock and she and Mari had been sewing all night. She had the forethought to bring one or two spares and for the Milan show, one more could be couriered to them from New York. She had come out of her nightmare only to feel the guilt and disappointment of letting not only her boss and the model down, but also herself. It was so out of character for her to lose something at such an inopportune time. She heard a knock on the door, *Grady,* she thought.

It was Moda, all bright eyes and gushing with excitement for the week ahead.

"Hello, how are you? How was your flight over?" She exclaimed.

"It was simply all right," answered Kascey. "Bad news. We lost the dress meant for you, so we were sewing all night and have come up with this one instead." She explained in a rush.

"Oh, I am so sorry to hear that." She did not know what to say and held her head down. Moda's eyes widened in shock.

"Thank you. It looks fabulous, really. I am sure that no one will notice. You are such a professional." Moda was pleased with the outcome as she spread the new piece with her hands, there were some differences, but the general mood of the dress was the same and it fit with the rest of the collection. "Look. I will go try it on," she said calmly.

She excused herself while Kascey and Mari felt so relieved. She then heard another knock on the door. She flung it open expecting Vasquez, and saw Grady.

Kascey was so relieved to see him and was overwrought from exhaustion, "Oh, I am so happy to see you." She hugged him as he was still confused from a long flight and from her reaction. It was not quite the response he was expecting and with quite a few people around.

"Hey, hey what is the matter? I am happy to see you too." He kissed her cheek.

"Moda's dress went missing and it has not turned up, and I have been up all night working on a new one. Vasquez is not pleased."

"Wow, wait a minute, a dress went missing. You mean *the* dress?" Asked Grady, and being a man of the world in the financial arena, he would read more into it than it seemed. "Look, you? You can't seriously think that it was your fault? I am sorry, but when was the last time you have lost a whole dress?"

"Oh, I guess you are right," she responded reassured to an extent, "Come in and sit down." She was now beginning to see the clarity of it and she was so happy that he would fly all that way just to be with her. He was right, she had never been careless in the past, and it was out of her possession for so many different periods of time. She hoped that Vasquez saw it that way.

"Hi, Mari. How are you?"

"Oh, well, I know you have heard, but under the circumstances, I suppose I'm fine." Mari reasoned and was glad that they had a solution.

At that moment, Moda reappeared wearing the new dress. She was beaming with pride and it was flattering on her.

"What a gorgeous gown!" Mari exclaimed relieved.

"Yes, it fits. It suits her. Mari, please hand me that pin pad and the scissors. We need to adjust the drooping collar." To Kascey, Moda had a shifting physique, and the dress was a bit billowing.

"Oh, it is fine," Moda reassured her.

"I just need to get rid of this gaping here near the shoulder. I cannot believe it. I just cannot believe it," Kascey was still in shock.

"Hi Moda, how are you?" Greeted Grady who was now sitting perplexed on the sofa.

"Hi, Grady, I feel much better now. I see that you are joining us this week. Fabulous. Have you had enough excitement?"

"I am sure the dress will turn up soon. If not, something is wrong. But yeah, I am glad that I can offer some support in and around a few meetings."

"You did not tell me that you had a few meetings?" interrupted Kascey.

"Well yes, sorry. I was meaning to tell you, but I figured you would be at the show anyway. Besides, I will be there for the final viewing," he said rather apologetically.

"Oh, okay, if you put it like that, dear," she responded laughing and just overloaded with too much work to think about it anymore.

There was another knock, and this time it really was Vasquez, who was still upset over the incident.

"Hello all, Moda. How are you? Do you like the new dress? It fits well." He tugged at the looser pieces of material and looked over at Kascey to adjust it. "What would I do without my right hand?" he asked as he looked at Kascey appreciatively and understanding all that she had been through. He was knowledgeable and knew that it was more than what met the eye and not Kascey's fault. He had been in the glamour business for years, and accidents happened. He could not jeopardize a show and his reputation because of one incident.

Grady and Vasquez had only met once or twice. Their worlds were very different, but Kascey bridged that gap between them. The group laughed and chatted about the incident and the days to follow. Vasquez wanted to plan with Moda before the other models arrived for their fittings. She was his other asset, and he relied on her beauty and manner to perfect his collection.

Kascey and Vasquez met the models throughout the afternoon and addressed the details for the show. She was exhausted by the end of the day with no sleep, yet she still had the time for a quiet dinner with Grady. The two strolled arm in arm along the Rue Rivoli in the mild Parisienne air and ate in a classic French restaurant where they studied an extensive menu. Kascey decided on the filet of sole, and Grady chose the chicken filet with fries. He was starving from the long day and managed to get some rest while Kascey worked. She knew that she would have an early evening, however, enjoyed the minute time that they shared until planning another meeting the following evening.

Still disturbed over the missing bag and feeling jet lagged, she nestled close to him during dinner for comfort. Grady sympathized with her and said, "Please do not worry about the bag. You have too much to think about on this trip. If you wing this trip, there will be no more chances. You have to move on from it. Just be on guard that risks can occur." He coached her.

"I know, I know, but it is perplexing. I am pretty sure I had it with me the whole time," she rationalized.

"I know, but you have to let it go. You have sorted the issue, now save your energy for tomorrow," he empathized.

"Thank you for being so understanding—and thank you for coming. I really appreciate your support."

"You are very welcome. I am so happy to be here. I am glad that I came when I did." He was right, he was not sure how she would cope without him, and it actually sealed the deal for him that it was almost time to start thinking about something more concrete with her.

"Let's change the subject," she said. "Who are you meeting tomorrow?"

"I have to go to the office to meet some colleagues regarding a deal I am working on. On Tuesday, we are going to meet the clients and a prospective buyer on the offering," he replied. Knowing that there was so much more to it than that.

"Well, good luck, I will see you after that," she continued excited about their plans.

"I know. I am looking forward to it," he said beaming.

They were in such a romantic city, and they planned to spend some time together albeit during a most hectic period.

Chapter 5
THE MONDAY CATWALK

The day had arrived and Vasquez was prepared for it. The sun rose dimly on a mild February in winter. It would soon be March and the continental spring was beckoning.

In the morning, Kascey was a walking zombie as she made last-minute preparations after dinner. She met Mari and Vasquez for a brief breakfast and then headed to the show in the center of town. Moda and Talia had gone ahead while the trio left with the suit bags and packages for the event.

The venue was filled with people as they hurried through to the changing rooms. The Paris show was more intimate, and Vasquez saw many faces he recognized. His rival Mario Leone was also present with his entourage and was used to being the center of attention. Vasquez's attitude was not as showy, but his talent was obviously noticed.

The atmosphere was energized as if in celebration. They immediately started to unzip the packages at their stations.

Moda, Talia as well as the rest of the models were having their faces and hair styled. Their faces were meant to be fresh for the season however, with severe cuts and styles distinguishing a more retro look. There were asymmetrical and strong-shouldered pieces for the season with a V neckline.

The outfits hung on the rack as the models took their pieces to wear. Many spotted them at first glance, and when ready, stood on queue and alert by the stage. The fast pace, and changes along with flashing lights from the stage, and the crowds' applause fueled Kascey. She kept it all moving until the last model exited the stage.

The audience showed their approval, and Vasquez and Moda took a casual stroll to the end of the stage along with a few models behind them. Vasquez bowed with one arm extended to the side as was customary while his head swooped down humbly for a quick moment. It was already three o' clock and they had finished the first show with the evening wear the following day.

Kascey checked her iPhone to see if more packages had arrived, and they had a nine o' clock delivery the following day. It was just in time for a few extra pieces to avert any more disasters.

"Congratulations to all of you. You were splendid!" Vasquez cheered as they gathered in the changing room. He hugged them all fully enthused from the reaction of the crowds to his outfits. He hoped that it would be the same for their evening wear the following afternoon. Moda was pleased with the result and threw herself into his hug and laughed, followed by Talia and also Kascey.

"Thanks to you," Moda exclaimed.

"Well done to you all," chimed in Kascey.

"Thank you," expressed Moda.

"No, thank you. Now get some rest for tomorrow. Do not overdo it this evening," warned Vasquez while still appreciative. It was his duty to look out for the group. He had known them for such a long time and also, they were a part of his company, and he was responsible for them. The event with the missing dresses had subsided. They all said good-bye until the following day.

The models were ecstatic that they could have a prance around Paris for the rest of the evening. They planned on sightseeing and shopping.

Vasquez had more of the collection to polish, and Kascey had a dinner planned with Grady. She missed his presence at the show and was excited to update him on her day.

* * *

Grady waited in the lobby in his suit and tie while the piano played a light number. Guests were beginning to return from their day tours and from the show when he glimpsed Kascey striding in with her suitcase. She had stayed behind to make sure it was all clear and to count several times before leaving. He looked at her exhausted face and pitied her.

She saw him and walked over to his seat and plopped on the settee.

"Hard day at work, I gather," Grady said as he rose to greet her.

"Yes, it all went well, very well." She responded proudly. We still have another day of shows."

"I see, how are you feeling?"

"Fine, just fine. I mean it was fantastic. You really should have been there," she responded trying to convince him to come again.

"Sorry. We had a long day at the office. I meet the clients in the morning, but I will be there for the last show—I promise."

"Great. I am looking forward to it."

"Any more about your bag?" he asked concerned.

"No, nothing. It has not turned up anywhere, not even on the airline," she informed him.

"If you are too exhausted, we can always do something else?" he offered.

"No, I am fine. I will see you in an hour. We'll have dinner near the Champs Élysées—my choice this time."

"Sounds perfect. I will see you then."

They rose after her short rest and walked to the elevators where he helped her with her suitcase. She wanted to prepare for dinner and had a lovely outfit planned.

He contemplated the enormity of their situation and felt like it was time to propose. He would hold off; she was too distracted, and he wanted it to be the right moment.

In her suite, she plunged herself on the bed and felt like taking a long nap, but she could not let him down. She turned on the TV and saw snippets of the show and their outfits being paraded down the catwalk. She grew more enthused and had a revelation. *Oh my,* she thought. *Is that really our work? Unbelievable.*

She found some vitamin juice in her shoulder bag and drank it in one gulp.

She dozed for forty winks and arose refreshed from her nap. It was amazing what twenty minutes could do, and she now had forty more to get ready for dinner. This time she chose a black, one-shoulder ensemble along with a red cashmere coat. She slipped on her pumps, applied her rouge and lipstick, and was ready for the evening.

They decided to stroll the short distance to the Champs Élysées, halting along the way and browsing the windows of the most famous fashion houses; all of which were known to Vasquez. She felt a sense of pride. It was only just a few years earlier that she had been a student in La Marise. She had wandered the cobblestoned pavement and discovered the nooks and crannies of the district where quaint shops were nestled.

"You have such a sense of style," he said. "I do believe that one day you can have your own fashion house. Just let me know—I can find the financiers for you. I promise you."

"I know. Thanks, but I am just not ready. Besides, Vasquez really needs me. We are halfway through the season, and I can put my plans on hold while he sorts out the financial aspects." She was appreciative of all that he did for her. She was an unknown in the country and he hired her—and he had faith in her. She would only move on when the time was right—and with his approval.

"I understand your reticence, but with the way the market is, you have to find your opportune moment. If there is another downturn, there will be no more financing. I am sure that you understand my hastiness. The money that is here today may not be here tomorrow. Investors want to realize the potential of their money today. You must think of the time value of money and a dollar today is worth more than a dollar tomorrow. Anyway, enough serious business. I am so looking forward to this little bistro."

He clutched her arm as they kept strolling and then followed up the Champs Elysees; then, down a side street, where they found their restaurant.

Kascey paused before entering the restaurant to admire the outside; she did not want to lose the moment. The city lights shone from the main road where the cars were still bustling. The evening had progressed and it was dark.

"Shall we?" he motioned as he opened the door for her.

"Why, thank you." She walked in first and he quickly maneuvered to the desk where he found the maître d' in attendance. He pronounced his name for him and the maître d' led them to their table. The atmosphere was beautiful, a proper bistro with the laced table cloths and a violinist.

"Wow, would you look at that?" she commented. "It is just as I imagined."

"Yes, it is great in here. I wish we had more time to go to the country or visit the south. I have heard so much about it. Now shall we take a look at the menu? Or do you already know what you would like?"

"Well, I must admit that I did peruse it online. So I basically know what I would like. However, I will take another look." She felt as though they were the only ones in the establishment.

Grady ordered the veal, and Kascey only wanted a seafood salad. She intended to splurge on the desserts, which looked divine. She had to sample the passion fruit crème brûlée.

"I have been thinking and I do not want to sound too hasty, but I think we have real potential," he said as he admired her sampling her appetizer.

"Thank you. I feel the same way about you."

"I know, but I think we can possibly become even more serious. Do you think that it can happen?" He was so concerned about her opinion.

"Yes, I think that it is possible." She was not sure where it was going.

"Okay, what I mean is, can you give me a hint? I cannot really see myself with anyone else. I am sorry to sound like a cliché." He could not be any more explicative.

"No, not at all. I feel the same way so, we should, what move in together?"

"Well, eventually, that would be a plan, of course you have a lease —but perhaps you should not renew your lease." He advised.

"I see, well the lease ends in the fall. Do you think that we will be ready by then?" she asked.

"Yes, I think so. I think that we should find a place. I know it sounds strange, but I just want to plan. You can think about it some more. You do not have to give me an answer tonight," he negotiated.

"I will think about it, and we can talk more back in New York. By the way, when is your flight back?" inquired Kascey.

"My flight is on Wednesday morning first thing and I should be at work by lunchtime in New York." He was dreading the ending of the trip but had to face the office and felt as though he had been gone for a long time.

"Well, I will miss you while I am in Milan after this."

"I know, but I will see you this weekend, right. Remember my sister's birthday bash? She is so looking forward to seeing you again.

"I know. I will not miss it for the world." She assured him. The two chatted over the remainder of dinner.

Kascey had to return to review the next collection that night and to finish any last-minute fittings. She was expecting Moda first thing and needed to calm Vasquez who was still unsettled about the dress. However, with Grady by her side, she was confident that it would go well. Their silhouettes were expressive in gesture while the mild winter's breeze refreshed the air.

Chapter 6

HECTIC MORNING

Kascey was already up and sipping her coffee in her suite when her phone rang. It was Vasquez all bright and cheery and ready for the grand finale.

"Are you ready?" he asked politely.

"Yes, more than ever. I cannot believe that it will soon be over."

"I know, and we have a few more shows, but I will have to make a quick trip back before Milan to meet you over the weekend there."

"Okay, I can cope with that," she responded professionally with the recent events still in her mind.

"I know. It is just that I have to deal with the last orders. Corrine is a bit inundated. Check on the missing bag," he stated.

"Oh I am so sorry about that, but this dress looks spectacular. We will have the replica finished by Milan, most definitely," she reassured him.

"Perfect. I always know that you can do it," he complimented. It was essential that she kept upbeat in order to have the confidence to finish the trip; he knew that Grady's arrival was a blessing in disguise.

"Let me know when the first model arrives for the fitting. We have a long day ahead."

"Surely, we do. Talk to you soon," she confirmed with him just before hanging up.

* * *

Grady was already in his car riding to a scheduled meeting with a client. The boulevard had such a serene and grandiose feel as he viewed the office building. He was working on a new deal and hoped that this offering would bring the international acclamation he desired. The buildings had Old World charm, iron gates near the entrance, and all the modern amenities in the interior. He enjoyed the continental flair and was so experienced that he felt as if he could fit right in.

He met his associates and had a lengthy meeting discussing the new Jacob Commerciale IPO. It was still in its initial stages and worth close to 60 million Euros. It would place him on the international stage. He looked at his watch, and it was almost 1:15 p.m. luckily, the meeting was tapering down and he could make it the short distance to the show's venue where Kascey was busily making her preparations.

* * *

At the venue, Moda was already dressed in the red ensemble. Kascey had the models placed in the color sequence of their dresses, with red, beige, and black silhouettes in a row. Vasquez was prepared to take his stroll with Moda for the finale while Kascey peeked across the stage to see if Grady's seat was taken. It was still empty at half past the hour. *No way,* she thought, *he promised me.* This time she was at the end of her tether.

She had to remain focused and a bit understanding. After all, it was a long way to travel for him not to get anything done on his own. She peeked again and there he was, diligently seated as if he had been there the whole time. Her heart fell as she eyed the person in her life and felt proud.

The models filed out as she and Vasquez cheered them on. There was movement in the dresses and the fast pace sent it all reeling out of proportion with the applause and the flashing lights from the photography. Moda's walk was the last as the crowd applauded. Kascey was relieved that it had all worked out.

Vasquez was ready to take his bow and grasped Moda's hand as she filed in, also assembling a few more of the ladies to trail behind. Vasquez felt exhilarated at this moment; out of all of the European shows, this one was his favorite because of the affinity he felt to this market. The crowds applauded as he took his customary bow and letting loose of Moda's hand, he waved and returned to the dressing rooms.

"Well done, everyone, well done. We are done," he said clapping his hands and meeting Kascey with a hug. "Thank you, thank you," he said over and over.

"You are so welcome, and thank you," Kascey responded.

They all gathered in closer to relish in the moment of a show well done.

"It all worked out well in the end. I knew it." He was relieved that it did work out, that the dress passed the ratings, and they were about to go on another excursion to another country. Moda thanked Kascey for her help of which Kascey was appreciative however, Moda was part of the brand and it was also to her that they were grateful.

"Now, everyone, let us all move out of the way and get going back to the hotel. We have a little soiree planned to finish the trip," Vasquez announced.

"What soiree, I did not know?" Kascey asked.

"Oh, it is meant to be a surprise. Mari and I put it together last night—just a few hors d'oeuvres and drinks in the suite to get us through a long day."

"Thanks. I'll tell Grady, but in the meantime, let's pack these things and get them back to the hotel." Kascey was so pleased, and even more so that Grady was able to see her work in action. He was astonished by the reception of her work and had big dreams for Kascey, beyond what she could imagine.

* * *

The suite was decorated with streamers as the hotel staff awaited their return. Mari ordered the most exquisite canapés as sparkling drinks sat on little silver trays to be served. They were expecting about fifteen people, and it was fully organized.

Kascey was impressed by the quality of the service.

Grady tried to fit into the fashion world, but the new deal was on his mind. He could not wait to get back to his desk to do the real planning.

"What did you think of it today?" Kascey asked.

"Oh, it was amazing. I cannot believe how well it went. You should be very proud. And the dresses, the crowd loved them," responded Grady as he drew her closer with one arm proudly. "I am truly impressed by it all, dear."

"Thank you. Where would I be without you? You are always to supportive."

She was right; he is a blessing to her as she is to him.

The evening passed as they all laughed and chatted about the last few days and how quickly they went.

Grady had an early flight to New York, and Kascey had the remainder of the week in Milan before getting back to her welcoming walkup in the west village.

The two spent their last evening in Paris before returning for coffee in the lobby. There was such a burst of artistic sophistication as Kascey reminisced over the past few days with him. They laughed and chatted knowing that for the next few days they would be a part, and she would spend more time on the continent while he would return to his everyday life in New York. He felt as though he had been gone for a very long time, and that it was very far away.

"Well, this is it—until next weekend. I have so much to do when I get back," he said.

"Oh, take it in stride. Plan it all on the way back," she advised.

"Don't forget Lucinda's bash on Saturday night. I know that you will be tired, but it is so important to me." Grady reminded her because he was very close to Lucinda, if it had not been for her, he would not have met Kascey.

"Of course, I would not miss it for the world. I am so looking forward to it." She was relieved that the trip went well and that there were only a few more days left of her travels.

"Now, I am sorry. It is time to get a move on. I cannot miss that flight," he said.

"I know, but a few more moments—I just want this to last." The lobby was alive and they had to unwind with dainty tunes being played in the background.

Chapter 7

BACK TO NORMAL

After Grady's plane touched down just before lunch, he quickly cleared customs and headed downtown. His office was bright and airy; Norma had been in to straighten it a bit. He disliked when she did that because he could never find anything. So he tucked into his desk drawers and started to rearrange things back to where they were. His PC was on, and the messages flowed in continuously.

"Welcome back," Norma greeted as she came in with a few more files.

"Thank you. It is great to be back."

"I hope so. Here are some documents for the new IPO. Please let me know if there is anything that I can do, and here's a reminder for your meeting after lunch."

"Thanks. I will get on it," he replied concentrating on his emails.

They started, *Hello Grady, hope that you got back safely, need the financials for Jacob Commerciale,* wrote Germaine from the Paris Office. He replied, *I will get right on it. Sure thanks, had a safe trip back.*

Then there was one from Kascey, *hi just checking that it all went okay, call me later.* He replied, and then one from his mother, *Just wondering how it all went, any news?* So he replied, *not yet Mom, will keep you posted.*

He had a meeting to prepare with his managers in an hour. It was an update on his curriculum in France, and would be buried in paperwork until then.

II

Kascey had arrived in Milan and checked her e-mails constantly. Vasquez was not due to arrive until the following morning, just in time for the show the following day, Friday. Then they were all due to leave on Saturday. She checked her e-mails; one was from her mother, Mabel.

Hi, dear, just checking in to see how it all went—any news. Her parents were expecting her to be engaged at any time. *Your father and I are coming to New York next weekend, and it would be great to see you. We have a hotel booked. Let us know when we can go to dinner or see a play. Looking forward to seeing you. Mum.*

Gosh, she thought, *it is all happening so fast.* She knew that Grady would want to see them; she had to inform him. She was excited to see her parents again. She had not seen them since the holidays, and she needed to confide in them about her plans.

She also received an e-mail from Grady who had just ended his meeting with his supervisors, he sounded cheery, *great,* and he got in safely.

She replied to her mother's e-mail and then Grady's while waiting to have a wonderful meal in the ancient Italian city. Milan was full of atmosphere and history and was coupled with the modernity of their mission. By the following day, the entire entourage had arrived. It was business as usual for the rest of the trip. Vasquez and Moda made the customary finale bow, and Saturday's flight was around the corner. Relieved, she packed and waited for its arrival.

When it did arrive, she was one of the first to be ready for the airport. It was no shock that they were all exhausted, as they climbed on board with all of their parcels and hand baggage. She sat next to Vasquez who went over the entire week with her. They discussed orders and the next few days back in New York before they got some much-needed rest. The stewardess woke them for a meal just before landing.

"Wow, I cannot believe that I slept almost the whole flight?" She remarked.

"I know. It has been a tiring week, and of course coupled with the jet lag, it is good that you have done so."

"Yes, Grady's sister is having her birthday party tonight. At least I will be alert," she said sarcastically.

"I can't wait to get back to my family. They always seem to be so affected when I leave. The minute I return, they all play normal."

"I know. I suppose it is a sacrifice of the profession. I miss having Daphne around too. At least you get some time over the weekend."

"I suppose, whatever I can do until the next trip. Which now will not be until the fall," he said smiling. It was true; he was beginning to feel guilty that he was leaving them for such a long period of time.

The plane landed, and the company disembarked. The other passengers looked on inquisitively as they drew so much attention.

Kascey took a cab to the Village and called Grady, "Hi, I am in and on my way to the apartment. See you in a few hours."

"Great. How was the flight?"

"It went well. I slept for most of it and can't wait to check on the apartment. Nathalie was looking after it in my absence. I will call you before I leave. I want to get dolled up for the occasion."

"Sure, talk to you soon. We are all looking forward to seeing you." On that note, he hung up. He was overjoyed that he had his companion back in the city.

Kascey pulled her luggage up the stairs to her apartment. She opened the door quickly and dragged everything inside the foyer. She placed the keys on the entrance table and walked through to inspect it. It was okay and clean. It actually was fresher than when she left it, and she had to thank Nathalie. She searched the fridge for a can of seltzer and gulped it down. Flights always made her so thirsty. She sat on the sofa and turned on the news. It was amazing how one could miss the little things after a long trip. She walked to the bags and unpacked immediately cherishing the little souvenirs she bought for her friends.

Fully unpacked, she got her outfit for the evening together. She chose her black velvet dress and patent leather slingbacks with a choker set of pearls. She figured that a nicely swept updo would suit the occasion. She settled on something minimalistic in comparison to all of the style and fashion that had flourished over the previous week. She checked her answer phone and there was just one message from her mother. She called her.

Mabel had a long day at the factory, but she was always happy to hear from her daughter. "Is that you, Kas? How are you? How was your trip?"

"Oh, it went well as usual. I had a great time with the company, and Grady came to spend a few days in Paris. I am seeing him this evening. He is having a party for his sister."

"Well that sounds lovely. Any more plans, dear? Any wedding bells in the near future? I know that you are very close." Mabel pried a bit and did not want her only daughter to make any mistakes.

"Well, he is hinting at it. We shall see. I will keep you posted." She did not want to reveal too much as to set her up for a fall if it did not happen.

"I see, well keep me posted. Have a nice time tonight. Don't drink too much," she advised.

"Of course not. I never do," Kascey remarked.

"Your father and I are coming next weekend and we will be staying in midtown. We really want to have dinner with you and Grady, so let me know of somewhere nice. Perhaps the concierge can tell us. It has been so long since we have had a trip there."

"Yes, it has been very long, but I can find a place I am sure you will both like." She reassured her mother until it was time to hang up and get dressed. The time was flying and it would soon be 8 p.m.

"Okay. Bye, dear, and see you soon."

"Bye, Mom. See you soon."

She felt a pang in her chest from homesickness. After all the years, it still hurt to know that they were so far away and that their lives had diverged. She did not know if they would every fully combine again, even though they were in the same industry. Perhaps Grady was right, maybe she needed more flexibility to locate herself strategically close to the factory and utilize their services.

When Kascey arrived, Grady was waiting near the entrance. "Hey, you look smashing. You really do," he greeted his girlfriend.

"Thanks—so do you. I love that suit," she flattered him. She liked his navy blue suit, especially when he spiced it with a colorful shirt for the occasion.

"Thank you. Shall we?" He motioned to the bar area where there was a part sectioned off for the group.

"What a splendid venue. I think it is perfect—not too loud and elegant. Where is the birthday girl?" Kascey remarked.

"She is right over there standing to the left." Grady directed her.

Lucinda was giggling and laughing with a group of friends with a glass in her hand. She appeared like a golden girl. She was embellished in conversation and had such vibrancy. She looked over and waved to Kascey.

"Hi, Happy Birthday!" Kascey drew nearer and gave her a hug.

"Thank you, thank you for getting back on time; it is so nice to see you again."

"Oh, it is my pleasure, truly." The two never had a problem expressing their appreciation for each other.

"I see, well great. These are my friends, Claire and Trudy. I don't think that you've met."

"No, I do not think that we have," stated Kascey as she extended her arm to shake theirs.

"Pleased to meet you," Claire remarked.

"Yes, pleased to meet you. I hear that you are a designer," Trudy said.

"Yes. I have been away this week at the shows. It was really invigorating."

"Sounds great. I am so jealous. I wish that I had a life like that," replied Claire.

"Oh, it sounds more than it is, really," stated Kascey trying to be a bit unassuming. She handed the gift to Lucinda, "Here, I bought this for you my last day in Milan. I hope that you like it."

"Thanks so much. You shouldn't have, but I am glad that you did. I am sure that it is perfect."

Just then, Grady took Kascey over to meet a colleague from the office.

"Hi, excuse us, I just want you to meet someone from the office, Claude. Claude was the financial controller at the firm and he had told him so much about Kascey, they really wanted to make her dreams of her own fashion house a reality.

"Claude, this is Kascey," he introduced them.

"Hello, Kascey. I have heard so much about you. I hear that you have been traveling to France and Italy?"

"Why hello, Yes. I did not know that you were from Europe."

"Yes, I have been here five years now, but I know Grady from the Paris office. I must say that you are quite remarkable."

"Why, thank you. That is a compliment. Did you hear that, Grady?"

"Yes, you sure are. Thanks." Grady was sure to be on the mark with that comment to avoid any issues.

Kascey smiled as she knew that Grady was a real sport and was not the jealous type. She talked to the group along his side. More of Lucinda's friends arrived, and the venue grew crowded. Kascey could hardly move and left the bar area to stand closer to the edges to avoid the traffic. She was tired, and it was almost 4 a.m. where she had just been. However, she hung in there with him by her side. He relished the moment by taking it all in around her.

It was near half past one and she decided to make her exit. She had work piled up for the week.

Grady escorted her to the taxi and set her in while he closed the door behind her.

"Bye. Get some rest. I really hope that you had a nice time," he bid her goodbye for the evening.

"Yes, surely. It was fantastic. See you for lunch tomorrow?"

"Sure thing. Bye—and thank you for coming."

"Okay, dear. Do not get up to anything. See you tomorrow," she said.

The taxi sped down to the village where on a quiet tree lined street, her building was situated. She opened her front door and climbed to her floor. Her apartment welcomed her and her antique Queen Anne style bed was prepared for her arrival as she settled in and fell into a deep slumber.

Chapter 8

NEW NEWS

Vasquez was in the fashion house bright and early on Monday. He was refreshed after an amazing weekend with his family. His sons were ecstatic to see him and had a list of achievements to share from the past few days. He thought of the lovely Sunday afternoon. They sat near the fireplace and played games in the lounge room on a crisp winter's morning.

He had an afternoon meeting with his financial advisors. He sat at his computer and went over the new orders for the shows. He was overcome with pressure; Marley's Department Store had placed in an order for two hundred fall outfits. Another one had ordered three hundred. He would have to use his outsourcing again because there was no way that it could all be done in time.

Kascey arrived a few minutes later and acknowledged all who were present. She had organized her day and sat in front of her computer. She tried not to bother Vasquez who was in a disgruntled mood, which was customary when he had an appointment with his financial advisers. The phone continued to ring off the hook with clients who placed orders and needed them expedited.

Things were now back to normal as it was so quiet the previous week. The morning proved to be no different as they all sat diligently to reap the rewards of a trying past few weeks.

Kascey browsed the off-the-rack collections, which always came up with interesting products after the show. She viewed the listings. She could not believe her eyes when she saw an idea lifted from the grand finale dress that went missing. It was a carbon copy of their design. Her chest sank as she felt pins and needles all over. She looked over at Vasquez conscientiously at his work, *Oh no, how do I tell him?* She grew nervous. It was not how she expected her morning to unravel. "I cannot believe this!" she exclaimed, hoping that someone would hear.

"What do you mean?" Mari asked.

"This dress looks just like ours—the one that went missing," she explained.

"You cannot be serious. Let me see," she said as she rushed to her desk.

"You are so right, Vasquez. I think we found the dress!"

Vasquez looked up by what he had just heard. Curiously, he strode to Kascey's desk and looked at her screen.

"Ah, look at it, you see! This is what makes me annoyed—when people do things like this. Now I know someone lifted that dress, and I am going to make a full report. Right here."

"I am so sorry," Kascey responded despondently, and was back in a place that she thought that she had gotten over. "I cannot believe it. Someone must have been targeting us."

She dreaded to think that there was more to it. Perhaps it was just a coincidence after all. *How could they come up with the dress so quickly?* She thought. They attempted to find the origination of the web site but to no avail.

Vasquez had another thing to get through before the meeting with his advisers and he was so very disappointed. A dark cast overcame the company as they all tried to grapple with the mistrust and betrayal. At this point, it was too soon for Vasquez to pinpoint the culprits because they had covered so much ground before attending the shows in so many places. They knew that they were dealing with someone who was very familiar with their movements. Vasquez perished the thought of an inside job. They were such a small company—and he knew they all were loyal.

* * *

The afternoon brought even more grief for Vasquez who arrived after a long lunch rather moody. The financial forecast did not look bright. There was so much competition. It was tough for a fashion house such as his with unique specialized items when there were mass producers on the Internet. Kascey's factory was one of them. To him, it was not the industry he knew but he knew that he had to change with the times. Therefore, he needed a new strategy—or else his company would not survive.

He did not know how to break the news to everyone. *What a time for them all.* He thought. He intensely sat and complied with the orders even personally thanking his clients for their loyalty, but he knew that he would have to completely change things and hire more staff in the technical and shipping fields to survive. He resolved to enter the mass retail marketing to save the company. For Kascey, this was not a new concept but one on which she had been raised.

* * *

Grady had a long day at the office. The Jacob Commerciale offering was in its final stages with a date for the following week. It all worked so quickly in his world. He had a lovely lunch at a restaurant near the park on Sunday and in the cold air headed to work soon after. Kascey had informed him about her parents' imminent arrival the following weekend. He decided to speak privately with them about his intentions while he had the chance. At lunch, Grady was still a bit under the weather from his sister's soiree, but he knew he had work.

Monday presented itself as a new day and he had the offer under control. He and Claude worked all morning. He called Kascey, "Hi, sorry.

I have been in meetings all morning, but I have a minute to see how you are doing?" He apologized.

"That's okay. We have been a little busy—and so much has come up from the shows. We think the design from the dress was lifted—probably from the actual dress in the bag. Can you believe it?" She explained.

"No, I cannot believe it, but isn't this a bit common? After they have seen it in a show, someone goes and copies it?" He asked.

"Yes, but this is a bit soon. Besides, it is more like the dress that went missing."

"No way. Are you serious?" He became more shocked.

"Yes, I am serious. Vasquez is going to take legal action," she informed him.

"You bet, I cannot believe it. It was on purpose? And here you were thinking that it was your fault when it was sabotage," he concluded.

"Yes, it sounds as if it is—and that does not make me feel any better."

"Oh, it will be fine. At least you are a few steps closer than you were last week to finding out whoever was behind it."

"I know. Whoever is behind it is the lowest of the low," she chided.

"I am sorry to hear it. If you need anything, just call me—even if I am in a meeting. Okay? I am always here for you."

"Sure. I will call you later." She hung up and got back to work, but she tried to trace her steps and wondered *When could it have happened? Did it ever make it on the plane?*

Grady was certain that something untoward had occurred—and that she should not blame herself. She had been targeted, and it was up to him to protect her. She had now suffered the detrimental blow of the ramifications from the incident, more so Vasquez. He got back to work on the IPO.

* * *

Vasquez took the expressway back to Westchester where he approached his safe home nestled in the snow. The trees were still spiny, but soon would be bearing leaves as it was soon spring. He parked his car in the garage and entered his home to the loving arms of his wife and children. Daphne had prepared a lovely oyster and pesto penne and flan for dessert. Each night she had a theme for the boys. Jose and Miguel were on the carpet of the sitting room rolling their trucks and personifying their action men.

He smelled the aroma and said, "Hello, dear. I am here."

"You are right on time for dinner," she said as she looked up from over the tantalizing pots of food.

"Wow, it smells *so* good," he said as he gave her a hug.

"Thank you," she was pleased, "Really? What is that for? She asked surprised.

"I will discuss it with you later," he explained.

"Okay. Is something wrong? You look exhausted?" she asked concerned.

"Yes, I mean it is under control. I had a meeting with my advisors. I need to make changes, but the new dress was swiped. We saw the design on the Internet; they even have new colors." He could not believe the absurdity of it all.

"What? Are you serious? I am so sorry to hear that? She responded more shocked. "It could not have happened at a worst time," she said.

"I know. Let's not dwell on it. We can talk later when the children have gone to bed. I just want to have a nice meal and relax with the children. Where are they by the way?"

"They are in the sitting room waiting for you and playing. I have been keeping an eye on them," she reassured him.

"Good. I can't wait to see them," he said as he exited.

He walked through to the sitting room adjacent to the dining room and saw them with their toys.

"Papa!" Miguel exclaimed.

"Hello my sons. How have you been?"

They looked up at him and nodded as they raised their toy trucks for him to view.

"I see. Nice. Can I play?" Vasquez sat next to them and started to roll the trucks—in the same way he did when he was younger with his own father. He was in a sanctity with them and stayed for a few more minutes before washing up for dinner. He cherished their time together —what he was doing was for them and of no use without them. He had a grueling day to say the least and needed his family time. Their innocence provided the security he needed which gave him hope that he could solve whatever issues he was facing. He managed to tear himself away to assist with the dinner preparations.

After dinner, he sat with Daphne on the sofa and close to the country fireplace which crackled. He had tucked in the children and was aware that they probably were not sleeping at that point. Daphne looked at her husband concerned.

"So, what are you going to do?" she asked quietly.

"I have to enter a new market and get into mass marketing."

"And you are okay with that?" she asked cautiously and peering into his eyes.

"Yes, I am okay with it. I have resolved myself to the fact that it needs to be done. With the support of new staff, I know that it can be a reality." He was confident that it would pan out well, and felt reassured that his right hand designer was fully backing him.

"Okay. I will support you in whatever you decide." She meant it, it had been years since they had met when she was a model and she would not let anything destroy what they, especially he, had achieved. "Look, I am so sorry about everything. Please let me help you with this. I also know the industry. If there is anything you need, I am here for you."

"Thank you my dear. I can always rely on you. It has been that way from the start—and we have many more years." He patted her arm in gratification and felt one hundred times better as he knew he would once he had confided in her.

* * *

Kascey decided to order some video games and a movie rather than go out. She was not in the mood to celebrate, and they had plans with her parents at the weekend. Grady stayed late at the office and arrived at around 8 p.m. She decided to order in from the French restaurant in the neighbourhood. She ordered his favorite profiteroles. He deserved it after having two large IPOs in one month.

"Look what I got for you?" He managed to find a bodega still open and had purchased pink carnations and white lilies for the coffee table.

"My, they are perfect. Thank you so much. How very thoughtful of you." She wrapped her arms around him.

"It was nothing. I just wanted to make you feel better," he replied casually.

"Thank you anyway, they are beautiful, I do feel better." She looked at them as if she had seen nothing as beautiful the whole day. She had changed her persona to being very calm because she felt as if she could handle the seriousness of it all. If all else failed for her, he was right, it would soon be time that she started her own fashion house.

"Oh, it all smells so good. What have you got in there?" he asked.

"Some of your favorites. I thought a mini replay of last week would lift our spirits. I ordered from Chez Sybil. You will see all of our favorite treats."

"Why thank you, I really appreciate it," he continued as he plopped on the settee. "However, I think that I should be catering to you after such a hectic day—and your first day back after being away for weeks," he admitted feeling slightly guilty.

"Thank you, but it would really keep my mind off things if I kept busy and organized. The whole company is going to change. We will be mass-producing clothing, and the technological aspect will change as well. It will be like starting over." She knew what he was going to say, but she could not think about that. Her loyalty was with the company.

"Sure, I understand," he was dismissive so as not to stress her anymore. "All right. So, your parents are coming?" He changed the subject.

"Yes, on Friday, we will all have dinner. I know we will have a good time, and they are so looking forward to it." She could hardly wait, and thought about a seafood and steak restaurant close to the hotel so that they did not have a long way to go, weather permitting.

"Sounds perfect. I can hardly wait." He really meant it as he had a plan and really needed to ask Ethan for his daughter's hand in marriage.

"I know, me too. How did Lucinda like her party?" Kascey was inquisitive because it went so well and it must have been the talk of the town.

"She found it perfect, absolutely perfect. She is still talking about it—and so is everyone else. Hopefully, things will calm down soon."

"I'm sure they will calm down, but I am happy that it was a success." She finished the touches before the food arrived. "Honey, can you help me with this bottle?"

He went to the kitchen and helped her.

When the food arrived, he scoffed down the meal which was perfect. They relaxed on the settee and watched one of her favorite movies. He thought that he would give her the allowances that she needed because she had deserved them during their quiet evening.

Chapter 9
PARENT TIME

The week flew past quickly, and Friday's weather was milder. It was growing lighter earlier and New York knew how to embrace the spring. There was an optimistic feeling in the air, which was pleasanter as people went along their daily routine. Kascey's week was mundane; they practiced damage control over the dresses and the factory.

Grady was on the eve of his new IPO. Monday would be the day, and he waited with anticipation.

Ethan and Mabel had checked in by three and were waiting in the lobby when Kascey arrived. She left work on time to meet them, and Vasquez sent his best wishes. He knew how important their link would be in the future.

Mabel was the first to see her daughter wander in and look around bewildered.

The lobby had grown more crowded. She hardly recognized her as she had lost more weight. *What are the girls doing these days?* She thought. *They all look so slim; it must be the new vegetable health drinks.* She waved to Kascey to get her attention.

"Kascey, oh Kascey dear!" she called as she approached still not seeing her fully.

"Hello, Mum, Dad. How are you both?" She asked as she extended her arms.

They raised up to hug their only daughter who had been the center of their attention their whole lives.

"Dear, we are just great," started Mabel pleased to see her, while her father followed.

"Yes, Kascey, we are so happy to see you. Sit down so we can chat about everything," continued Ethan very concerned about his daughter's well-being. Overjoyed, because it had been since the holidays, she sat next to them and they talked about Europe, work, and the missing bag. She had come an hour earlier to catch up with them before Grady arrived. Mabel listened intensely as Kascey described a beautiful time with Grady in Paris and how supportive he was about the dress incident. Also, how he has a solution to her problems and has a business plan for her.

Mabel looked at Ethan as he nodded at what she was saying almost in agreement to what she was proposing.

Mabel said, "Actually, dear, we support you 100 percent in your decision to start your own company. We think that you have the talent and the ambition to see it through. This is something we have always expected—and we will always be there for you no matter what."

"Thank you, Mum. I knew that you would be understanding and supportive. You do not know how much it means to me to hear you say that when things have been so difficult for me. Grady feels the same way, but I am so accustomed to my everyday routine that I would need more than enough strength to get through this venture."

"Well, you have it from us. We still have contacts in the fashion district. We have suppliers we still use every day internationally. It is not such a mom-and-pop operation after all, and we can support you in whatever you decide." In whatever she decided, as always, he would be ready for it.

"I wish that things were better for you, dear, I really do, but in life these incidents occur, and you have to see the silver lining. Your independence has evolved from this situation." Mabel said.

Kascey knew she could count on them for the backing that she needed.

They sipped their drinks and listened to the Friday night band until Grady waltzed in cavalier.

Grady was confident he would achieve his objective and enjoy the time with her parents.

"Grady, how are you?" Kascey asked as she got up when she saw him approach.

He smiled and said, "Fine thank you. It is so nice to see everyone here. How was your flight?" He motioned toward Mabel who gave him a hug while Ethan shook his hand. Kascey gave him a warm appreciative hug for making it on time.

Ethan started, "It was just fine, and it is great to see you. I hear that you have been pretty busy. Have a seat and tell us all about it."

"Yes. Please fill us in on things," Mabel said.

"Well, the trip was fabulous. I must admit that I had to do a bit of work, but it was all in the adventure. We had a beautiful time, right Kascey?" he said as he looked over at her.

"Yes, that is correct. It was wonderful. We managed to eat out a few nights."

"Yes, that is right and probably put on a few pounds," Grady tried not to get too involved in exactly how it went to avoid discussing the dress incident which was still a sore subject." He looked over at her to see how she was holding up.

"Yes, it was beautiful, and all the shows went really well."

Mable and Ethan were rather amused by it all. They adored Grady and really wanted him to be their son-in-law.

"Well, we are so pleased to hear that. When are you all coming to Toronto? We would be happy to see you?" Mabel asked.

"Soon." Kascey looked at Grady who nodded in agreement, "Perhaps over the holidays. My schedule is almost booked until then. I think that would be fine."

"Wonderful, that would be great," Mabel was excited by the prospect already.

"Look at the time! We have been so busy talking that we only have fifteen minutes until our reservation," Ethan noted.

"Yes, we had better get going," Kascey said as they all got up.

"Okay, just let me settle this bill and I will be right with you." Ethan went to the counter hastily to sign it to the room while they waited a few moments.

"Right let's go," stated Kascey as they walked to the revolving doors of the entrance and to the restaurant a few blocks away. It was a perfectly mild evening for walking, and the two couples had a brisk walk to the restaurant.

Mabel was pleased as they approached because she had seen it many times but had not been in. Grady held the door as they stepped in. Mabel loved the weather and the authentic ambience of the restaurant.

"Hello, table for four?" asked the maître d'.

"Yes, I have a reservation for Kann," informed Kascey.

"Yes, perfect. Right this way," stated Becky.

The group followed her to the wooden cubicle for four and sat. Becky handed them their menus and offered her assistance before leaving.

"It is beautiful, Kascey. It is just what I imagined. How did you know so well?" Mabel commented.

"I just knew, it is a very popular restaurant and a crowd pleaser. My, look at the menu, they must have everything—even scallion new potatoes," said Kascey.

Kascey and Mabel got on smoothly and were so much alike. Grady admired their relationship.

"Yes, Kascey it is a fine choice, you knew just what we wanted." Ethan was always complimentary to her and a very laid back individual. He was a hard worker but avoided the fuss.

The group was famished. Mabel ordered the shrimp. Ethan ordered the cod. Kascey ordered the sole. Grady ordered the sirloin, which was what he had desired from the moment he had heard her suggestion. Their waiter Simon had returned with the drinks, and Kascey sipped a non-alcoholic drink. She wanted memorable moments with all of them. To her, it was an important evening as she was with the three most important people in the world.

They laughed and talked about everything ranging from the past to the present economy, Grady's IPO and Kascey's new plans for her business. Her parents were still young and were not going to retire for a few more decades. Mabel ordered the most divine dessert that looked like a float. Kascey received a separate spoon to dig in while the men ordered coffee.

Grady took the bill and asked, "Please allow me. It is the least I can do. You have come to my town," he said graciously. "It is my pleasure."

"Rightfully," teased Ethan, "but it would be all right."

"No, please. I insist," he said respectfully.

Kascey was so pleased that he took the bill. He was so well brought up and it was so appealing. She watched him as he handed Simon his credit card and then signed the slip.

Ethan was silent and amazed at his chivalry. He turned to Ethan, "Thank you for having dinner with us; the pleasure has been ours."

"Thank you for taking the time from your busy schedule. We are very appreciative and thank you for the dinner," he replied.

"Yes, thank you. It was delicious. It is so lovely to see you," Mabel added.

"You are welcome, now, Ethan. There is something that I need to discuss and I would like to see you after breakfast in the morning if that is all right," requested Grady.

Ethan could guess what it was all about and Kascey was astonished by his courage.

"Sure, Grady. That would be great. I am looking forward to it. Ring me from the lobby when you come—maybe at about ten thirty?"

"Perfect. I will see you then."

Kascey extended her arm and gave a curious look while she thanked him for dinner. He looked back a little boldly as if not to let her in on it either and smiled. Mabel, on the other hand, knew just what it was and was so excited. The couples left the restaurant and enjoyed another brisk walk before saying good-bye.

"Bye Mum, bye Dad, see you tomorrow afternoon," said Kascey as she waved. They had tickets to the theatre.

"Thanks. See you then, dear," replied Mabel.

"Yes, see you then," continued her father.

"Okay, bye. See you in the morning," stated Grady.

"Sure, see you in the morning Grady. Bye now, and thanks," said Ethan.

"Yes, thanks for everything Grady. See you soon," remarked Mabel.

Grady and Kascey then hopped in a cab and went downtown.

Kascey's parents had a perfect evening, and decided to sit again in the lobby for refreshments before going to the room. It looked so appetizing on a Friday evening. They enjoyed the bustling ambience as they reminisced over past times and holidays in the city when they were younger, and of how proud they were that Kascey had decided to take it on and pursue her dreams. They saw the city in a new light. There was a closer connection and knew that it would be for years to come.

Chapter 10

DAY OF HOPE

Ethan and Mabel had a wonderful buffet feast, which involved everything imaginable. Mabel had French toast and their favorite crunchy granola. Ethan had proper scrambled egg whites, turkey bacon, a whole wheat muffin, and yogurt. He felt a cringe of anticipation as he prepared to meet Grady.

"I suppose I had better wait down here. It is almost time," Ethan remarked slightly nervous.

"Oh, really? I suppose I should leave it to you both," she said jokingly and fully aware of what it was about.

"Okay, you have a great rest. I will see you in a bit."

Ethan waited in the lobby until he saw Grady's clean cut brown hair emerge from the revolving doors. He was wearing casual olive corduroys, a striped blue and white shirt with his long black cashmere coat. He saw Ethan and walked over to shake his hand.

"Hello. Thank you for meeting me this morning," he said as he motioned towards him and extended his arm.

"Oh, sure. My pleasure. I gather that it is all about Kascey—who is very important to us all," he added.

"Yes, it is," Grady replied as they sat in the lobby.

"Would you like some juice? Have you had breakfast?" asked Ethan.

"I am fine, thanks. I have eaten and am still a bit full from last night," responded Grady appreciatively. He knew that he had to be polite as he was asking one of the most important questions of his life.

"So, what is it? Is there something important?" asked Ethan inquisitively.

"Yes, there is something. I know that you are aware how close that Kascey and I have become and how much she makes me happy. I feel as though we are ready to take our relationship to the next level, and I would like your permission to propose marriage? If that is all right? He added a bit jittery, but with the same precision as he went after everything else in his life.

Ethan smiled to take the pressure off, "Well, we are aware that you both have a strong relationship, and I speak on behalf of my wife and I, that we would be delighted to have you in our family. We think that you are a straightforward and honest person, and that Kascey admires you. Of course, son, by all means." Ethan was direct with his statement and did not want Grady to have any doubts. Grady was the one and Ethan could see that. He felt like he had just let go of something very precious, and wanted it to be done right for the sake of them all.

"Thank you sir. I will do whatever it takes to make Kascey happy, whatever, I promise," he replied relieved and excited.

"I will hold you to that," replied Ethan now feeling emotionally confused because he had accepted the occurrence of her impending proposal, and had agreed to make her a happy woman with Grady.

Grady laughed, "Yes, please by all means, and I thank you and Mabel so much for this. I truly do." The weight had been lifted, and the ice had been cut as any tension had now subsided.

"Well, we appreciate your respectfulness. Now, I will go and tell Mabel the good news. We still have some time before we see Kascey and will manage to keep it a secret for a bit longer. You have a nice day—and see you before we leave." He got up to leave.

"Yes, see you soon and have a nice time at the theater this afternoon," replied Grady still beaming.

He was happy that he had gotten it over with and would get a ring as soon as he could. He hoped to propose the following Friday.

* * *

Kascey had fond memories of going to the theater in New York with her parents. She relished the long lines on Saturdays where they all waited with anticipation to see the Broadway show. This was no exception as she waited on 48th and Broadway for them in the cool air. They were already five minutes late. She saw a yellow taxi pull up as their familiar faces became apparent to her.

Ethan and Mable clambered out of the vehicle and waved to her as she walked over.

"Hi, sorry we are late. We got caught in traffic," remarked Mabel.

"Yes, we left early, but there was a line outside the hotel and then the traffic was stuck," Ethan agreed.

"That's okay. It is good to see you. Did you have a nice breakfast? How did it go with Grady?"

"It went well, didn't it, Ethan?" Asked Mabel.

"Sure thing. It all went very well," he replied with smirk.

"What? Something about me?" she asked.

"No, nothing, I mean yes. You are in capable hands, dear," joked Ethan.

"Oh, I see," replied Kascey not exactly sure what to make of it, however, slightly reading between the lines.

Her mother beamed at her, and from that look she could tell that something was up. *That Grady. I wonder what he was up to this morning,* she thought, although, she could take a guess by her parents' optimism.

"Now let's see, I have the tickets already; we can just join the line on this side," directed Kascey as her parents followed.

They joined a fast moving line as it was getting closer to show time. They took their seats and waited for the musical to start. She always felt so cozy waiting for the orchestra in the initial moments. It started with a brilliant chorus and was a wonderful performance. *Bravo,* she thought being moved by the music of the ensemble.

Afterward, they decided to have a snack in the theater district before meeting again for dinner. The weekend was soon over and they were off Sunday at mid-day. They walked to a café where they sat and had beverages and dessert.

"It was magnificent. I must tell Grady," she remarked trying to bring him back in the subject again.

"Yes, it was very entertaining. I thoroughly enjoyed that one," agreed Ethan.

"Good choice, Kascey, good choice. Do you remember all the times we came here when you were little?" Mabel asked.

"Yes, I remember, we had a fabulous time. It is no wonder that I decided to move back," commented Kascey.

"I know, you moved here and we are so proud of you. We had thought about it at some point, but decided on the factory being in Canada, didn't we Ethan?"

"Yes, at some point," he replied.

"So where are you thinking of going this summer? Anywhere nice?" asked Mabel.

"Yes, we are thinking about going to Cape Cod in August and then a weekend in Europe. I am so excited, but who knows since things are different at the fashion house."

"I know, but try to remain optimistic. There are so many opportunities out there for you," consoled Mabel to cheer her up.

She knew that it would not be for much longer that Kascey would be the happiest woman in the planet. She could not wait to get the call. The family talked for the rest of the afternoon before dinner which was going to be closer to downtown where she lived. It was still bright out and they headed back to get dressed for dinner again to celebrate what would be a momentous occasion.

* * *

Sunday morning was difficult as Kascey thought about her parents preparing for their journey home. They all had a lovely time at dinner in the Village and in Kascey's new home.

Mabel and Ethan enjoyed New York's authentic Italian cuisine and this one was located on Sixth Avenue not far from her apartment. The group talked and sipped coffee after dinner. A memory was forever sketched in her mind. She reminisced about the happiness and the joy they all felt as a family. She also felt so united with Grady as though he fit right in.

She looked out at the street where light snow had newly fallen. A few people were up and scavenging about on chores while she turned on the coffee pot and read the morning papers online. The headlines heralded the coming of spring, and the style section was full of brightly colored outfits. She thought of her company and the problems that it was having. Also, about the lifted designs for the dresses and how such a dirty trick had affected all of them, even her parents.

The phone rang. It was her mother, "Dear, we are just calling to say good-bye and that we had a lovely time. Please tell Grady that we wish him the best with everything—and that we hope to see him again soon."

"Bye Mom, and see you all soon. I hope you both had a nice time. It was a wonderful weekend, and thank you so much for coming. I will tell Grady that you have left and what you have said," she reassured her mother.

"Great! We will contact you tomorrow to let you know how it all went today. We are heading to the airport now and your father is just about to let the bell cap in for the bags," Mabel replied.

"Okay, well please tell him that I said bye and call me if you need me."

"Okay, bye dear." And she hung up. They rushed downstairs to check out and then to catch a taxi to the airport.

Kascey felt even more alone and needed to call Grady. She stared at the four walls and knew that she had to pick herself up again and get back into her routine.

* * *

Grady was already at the office and having to prepare for the IPO the following day. He had purchased the perfect solitaire diamond ring in platinum and was thinking about the right time on Friday to give it to her.

He picked up the phone to give her a call. "Hello, and how are you this morning?"

"Hi, I was just about to call you. I am very well and thank you for another lovely evening with my parents. They had a great time and look forward to seeing you again. They have left now and said bye...and good luck with everything?" She continued slightly perplexed.

"Oh, thanks. Yes, they must mean the IPO tomorrow and we are fastened down in work," he responded inconspicuously. Claude and I are in overtime on this project and probably are for most of the evening. I am sorry, but we will have dinner tomorrow night, right?" He suggested apologetically.

"Sounds good. Try not to work too hard." She was satisfied regarding his explanation and did not want to go over it anymore since he had so much on his mind.

"Right then, we will touch base later and have a nice day." He said goodbye and hung up the phone. It was time to get on with serious work, and he needed his team with him at the office.

* * *

Kascey took out her business plan and started to go over her sketches. They were drawings she had designed during her training in Europe and which would one day become a reality.

By lunchtime, her living room was filled with paperwork and was a mess. However, she was putting together the start of her company and her mind flowed with ideas until the afternoon.

She looked outside her window again and realized that she had spent the whole day working as the sun set at 6 p.m. She knew Grady was also working very hard and did not want to disturb him, therefore, she ordered sushi. It was just what she needed to remain focused.

Chapter 11
FLAT FALL

Grady had been excited all day in anticipation of the offering. It had been on the market for a few hours, and the sales had not picked up as quickly. He hoped for a turnaround by the end of the day. Claude kept ringing anxiously to keep him informed of any new events from the floor.

"I hear that it does not look good. The price has fallen another ten cents on the dollar, and now it is down 20 percent from the initial offering," Claude delivered the bad news.

"Any lower and there won't be any ROI—unless we can turn it around in twenty-four hours."

"I don't know. We shall see. The sellers are doing the best that they can. The bids are slower and lower than anticipated."

"What? We can't have it. Tell them to keep at it and to do whatever it takes!" Grady ordered.

"Okay, but I don't know if it will stay afloat much longer. Word is out that it may bust," advised Claude now broken.

Grady hung up disappointed because he did not see that one coming. He needed a bulk buyer, and he needed one right away. He was certain that the market would end on a low, and he had the job of saving Jacob Commerciale's offer from crumbling. He searched his connections for other hedge funds and needed an infusion of at least $30 million, which was relatively minor in his world. It did not look good for them, and it was to be avoided. News had gotten out that there would be a loss, and nothing could be done.

* * *

Kascey had an eventful Monday in the Garment District. Orders had to be shipped, and Vasquez was interviewing technical experts for his new online trading store. It was new ground for them; they were targeting a new part of the industry. He was also meeting with new marketing executives the next day, and Kascey was expected to attend.

She felt a bit disloyal because of what she had discussed with her family about the business and that she had been preparing her own collection for the next winter season.

Corrine interrupted her train of thought. "Remember that you and Vasquez have a meeting on Madison Avenue tomorrow at 10 a.m."

"Thank you. I have it on my iPhone," replied Kascey appreciatively.

"Well, what did you think about Robert, the interviewee today?" asked Corrine.

"I think that he looked very intelligent and very chic," responded Kascey.

"I see. That's great news, because I think Vasquez will hire him to work here."

"I see." Kascey was perturbed as to how she would know before her.

"Well, I overheard him speaking to Daphne on the telephone."

"Well then, if it is to be, we shall have to see then," responded Kascey not wanting to get too much into it with her in case she was inaccurate. "Look at the time. I must be off as it is late and I am meeting Grady tonight for dinner," she explained.

"Okay. Have fun tonight—and see you tomorrow," replied Corrine unsure of why Kascey seemed distant all day. Usually she was in a better mood after seeing her family, however; Corrine cast it aside as plain stress from the changes.

Kascey knew that Vasquez had more interviews to come. In particular, he had one with a new designer who was skilled in mass-marketing and sales at a retail fashion house. She had been made redundant by the downturn and was possibly a new work colleague for her. She had been to a design school in the city and also had a business degree from an Ivy League school.

Grady was waiting for her at the Mexican restaurant in SoHo. He looked worse for wear as she waltzed in a few minutes late at quarter past seven.

"Hello, darling. Sorry that I am late," she said as she leaned over to greet him.

"Oh, hello. Do not worry," he replied despondently.

"Okay, well this is a change of attitude. What happened? Is something wrong?" she asked.

"Yes, something major. The IPO did not go as well as we anticipated," he revealed and was taken aback.

"No? Well, that is strange. Try not to be too upset. It may be just temporary," she consoled.

"I mean, I am not sure if this offer will pick up at all," he admitted.

"Oh," she replied concerned. "I am sorry to hear that. Please do not blame yourself. These things are unpredictable. You tell me that all the time with the financial crisis," she replied.

"Well, who else is there? It was my project," he continued.

She was lost for words as she had never seen him look so bad. She did her best to change the subject, but it was no use. They had a very solemn dinner and then he was headed back to work.

"I am sorry. I probably should have canceled. I really did not want you to see me like this," he explained.

"No, please do not feel that way. I am happy to see you, and you know that I am here for you, right? Do not be ridiculous. We are a team, right?" She reassured him.

"Right," he responded still no more enthused. "Look, we will get in a cab, and I'll drop you home before I go back to work."

"Sure, thanks, and please try to cheer up. I know that you can do this." She tried to cheer him up, but he was so despondent and this was a new phenomenon.

"Okay, thanks, come on. I'll get the bill," he said distantly.

The two left their quaint restaurant where they have had many different types of conversations on different occasions and took a cab. He dropped her off at her door, and the taxi sped downtown. He had more work to do, and there were only a few more hours before the markets opened in Europe.

Kascey walked to her front door and settled in after a long day at work. She looked at the sketches still on the coffee table and sat down while slipping off her shoes. She went over her plans again and was certain that it would be a reality. She would stay with Vasquez until the summer and then start her new collection. If only she knew how to break it to him.

* * *

Meanwhile, Grady sat in his office overlooking the river and the city lights and peered at his computer. He waited for Europe to awaken via his screen. He searched for a plan that might work. It was only day two and perhaps, with some finesse, he could turn it all around. He studied the figures again and tried to find a solution. Perhaps it was time to give in.

* * *

Kascey arose with a burst of energy. She had meetings and an interview with Vasquez all day and wanted to be at her best. If she was going to leave, she wanted to do it so that he would be in a better position and they would stay on good terms. It was her endeavor to see him through this new phase so that she could start hers. She put on her navy blue suit, pumps, and a tailored silk shirt. She grabbed her patent leather portfolio and slingback purse and walked out.

Vasquez was already there bright and early and going over the figures and projections for the meeting. He was tense as it was new ground, and he needed direction. He knew that he would have to change his fabrics and have a more durable style to satisfy the average customer. He had to lower the cost in order to see the profits from the sales, and there were so many different ways of adding new suppliers, but at the same time he also needed more staff.

After a brief look over the agenda and e-mails, Kascey and Vasquez left for their appointment on Madison Avenue. He had used marketers in the past and would need advice on this new form of branding. He also needed one in-house. He wanted the transition to be as quick and as smooth as possible. "I suppose that they will have a full presentation for us," he remarked on the way to the meeting.

"I suppose, but I think we will have to tell them a bit more about your vision and see if our plans meet," she suggested.

"That is true. I do not need a plan being marketed to me, and then it is not what I really want. I have heard that story many times."

"I know, hopefully these will be different," she replied.

The firm was impressive as its large glass windows overlooked the city streets below. They met with three executives—Matt J. Tuder, Tom Q. Harrest, and Cynthis Maiyz who went over the proposal. They also elicited information about Vasquez's vision. Much of the morning was spent looking at PowerPoints and explanations of strategies, shares, and niches. It was clear that he would be targeting a more medium household income and a younger market. At the moment, his was a more sophisticated market niche.

Vasquez also knew that he would need younger designers and new contacts at the fashion magazines which catered to them. It looked as if it would be a complete overhaul, and it would be a challenge. Unfortunately for Kascey, it was beginning to sound too much like her vision, and that would be the pivotal point for whether she would leave sooner.

Cynthis started to conclude the meeting, "So, I do hope that this presentation and our proposals have been useful. Please let us know if you have any questions about the presentation or if there is anything more that you need to discuss. We have seen a number of companies change course due to the shift in the markets and have experience in helping you achieve your goals." She was driven, precise, and coordinated in her thinking.

"Thank you, Cynthis, and thank you, Tom and Matt for your presentation this morning which has simplified my vision and made my objectives more achievable," responded Vasquez.

"If I have any more questions, I will get back to you."

"You are very welcome, and it was nice meeting you both. I hope we get a chance to speak again soon," concluded Cynthis as she and the other men shook Vasquez's and Kascey's hands. The two took the elevator to the lobby and started to walk along the avenue.

"That was splendid. I cannot believe how thorough that presentation was. They left no stone unturned," commented Kascey.

"I know. They were excellent, and I was very impressed. I think I will go with them. We have to get started on these plans," he responded more optimistic than the week before.

"Yes, I think that it is a good idea and they will really steer you in the right direction," she responded with enthusiasm.

"Now, come on let us hop in a taxi and get back to the studio because there is an interviewee coming in this afternoon." With a quick wave and a fast stop by one taxi, they were in and heading to the Garment District for the next appointment.

The others were eagerly awaiting their arrival and listened intently to the summary of the meeting. At this moment, they could also envision the objectives and thought of useful ways to fulfill them.

Vasquez and Kascey ordered in a few sandwiches for lunch and looked over the portfolio of the next candidate. Charlene M. Quiy had been a designer with a large department store and was in the niche they wanted to target.

She arrived on time squarely at two o' clock and they were relieved to have the extra few minutes to prepare. She looked around the floor filled with admiration and gave them both firm handshakes. She was confident and conservatively dressed. She spoke with an upper-class New England accent, perhaps due to her studies there. Charlene sat and listened intently to Vasquez's list of requirements and nodded in understanding.

She detailed her story, which explained why she was free and how she achieved her goals at work. Vasquez was impressed with her, which was obvious by his demure behavior and his reserve as he listened to her. She also went through her new portfolio of ideas and explained why the market could use such a collection, and how to mass-produce it for the average consumer.

Kascey also became impressed as she smiled and nodded in acknowledgement. It was clear that Charlene was right on track and that she shared their vision. The pair stood and extended their hands to Charlene when she was done.

"Thank you very much for coming. We will definitely get back to you in the next few days after we have discussed a few things," Vasquez explained.

"Thank you for having me. Please let me know if there is anything else that I can provide to you," she responded as she shook their hands and smiled at them.

After she left, Vasquez turned to Kascey. "What do you think?"

"I think it all sounded great, I mean she is experienced in what we need right now and she has a sincere personality. I think that she would be a good fit."

"Yes, I think so as well. Let me go over her resume, and then we will get back to her." Vasquez had a long day and was ready to head home.

Kascey was relieved that this had fallen into place. He had found someone who he could work with and could eventually replace her if she left. She had to tell Grady the good news. *Oh no, Grady, dear me.* She had forgotten about him all day because it had been so hectic and it was already past three. She knew that he was having a wretched day and gave him a call.

"Hi, Grady. How have you been? I am so sorry that I did not call sooner. I have been in meetings all day," she explained.

"I see. That is okay. We have been busy all day too. The IPO has fallen flat, and we are recuperating from the loss." He looked ruffled as if he had not slept a wink.

"Oh no. I am so sorry to hear that. I can see you later if you wish," she offered as an appeasement.

"I am fine—maybe tomorrow. We are busy here just sorting this out. It is a real mess," he explained and nothing could be done to make him feel better.

"All right. I am here if you need me. Just call. Bye." She signed off up feeling very guilty and disappointed with herself. She had no idea how to cheer him up. She got back to work and to her new sketches for the holiday season. They would be her last for the company, and she wanted them to be spectacular.

The day came to a close and she picked up her belongings and took a taxi to the West Village.

Nathalie had arrived at the same time, and the two ladies opened the front door and climbed the stairs.

"Hello, how have you been?" asked Kascey.

"Very well, thanks. It has been a tough day at work, and I am glad that it is over," she responded. Nathalie was in advertising at a large firm in lower Manhattan and house sitter for Kascey.

"Great. Mine was busy and I am glad that it is all over."

The two placed the keys in their locks and turned the keys.

Nathalie turned to her and said, "See you over the weekend. I will stop by on Saturday afternoon after my errands to talk more."

"That sounds great. See you soon. I can't wait to fill you in on details." Kascey closed the door behind her and put down her things. She waited for Grady's call, and to be frank, she did not know if he felt up to anything after his mood earlier that afternoon. Perhaps she would just go to the kitchen and prepare something light for herself. It was something that she had not done in a while as she was used to being with him in the evenings, and he hardly let her near a kitchen.

Chapter 12

AT WEEK'S END

Friday had come at last and it was business as usual. Moda had stopped by to go over more fittings for the new collection, and Vasquez was busy preparing for the new staff. They created new stalls for them.

Kascey wondered what it would be like to have new people and hoped for the best. She felt excited and exhilarated at the same time to be turning a new phase for the company.

Moda stayed for most of the afternoon. "I think this apparel is fabulous. I love how sheer it is," she remarked.

"Yes, it is more like for a fancy evening party over the holidays. I think that they will be in several colors and also a bit more durable in ready-to-wear," explained Kascey.

"I shall be wearing it. We have charity events in the evenings around the holidays," replied Moda.

"That would be great. I am sure that Vasquez would be pleased."

"So, any plans this evening?" asked Moda.

"Yes, Grady and I are having dinner at La Monument. I am so relieved because he has been in a wretched mood over work all week. He has told me to wear something special," she responded, not knowing quite what was planned.

"I see. Have fun. Remy and I have an anniversary party. His brother has been married for ten years now."

"Really, that is a real achievement. I hope you have a fantastic time," responded Kascey.

"I know. He has been looking forward to it all week. So how can I not? Any more news regarding the missing bag?" She disliked bringing up the subject.

"No, no more. Besides with the designs being lifted, it means that I have to come up with more just to appear original. We still have not gotten over it," she responded sadly.

"I know. It is terrible, just terrible. I cannot think of who could do something like that. I feel like it was sabotage," replied Moda.

"It sure was, and we have paid the price," commented Kascey unenthused.

"Very well then. I have to dash and have something to discuss with Vasquez. By the way, we have a new designer coming I see?" asked Moda.

"Yes, we do have a new person, Charlene, and I am so glad we have found someone. Vasquez has plans to extend the production in Asia, and we know that she would be perfect for that enterprise." She was glad to change the subject.

"Great. I cannot wait to meet her. See you next week!" concluded Moda.

Kascey looked at the time and did not want to be late for dinner. She wrapped up her work and by six o'clock, she and the rest of the staff had left the building. It was still light out, and everyone felt a sense of change and renewal. Their spirits were optimistic—and they could finally see through the formidable clouds.

* * *

Grady wore his best navy blue suit which she always liked, a striped gray and blue tie, and a white French-cuffed shirt. He donned the cufflinks she had given him. He had a very expensive item in his upper coat pocket and guarded it with his life. He straightened his tie in the mirror and picked up his door keys. As he left the building, he exhaled the fresh air and took a taxi to midtown.

Kascey wore a silk cocktail dress with bold patterns and a string of pearls. She had a thirties motif with a clutching fishtail hemline and white lace gloves. She covered her ensemble with a beige coat and left her building.

Their taxis arrived simultaneously, and they greeted each other in front of the five-star French restaurant and walked in.

She was taken aback by his demure mood and thought that he had not gotten over the eventful week.

"Hello. How have you been?" he asked sincerely.

"I have been just fine, but I have been concerned about you." She said as she kissed his cheek.

"No need to be. I am fine. These things happen. Seriously, there is a first time for everything," replied Grady.

"Okay, but I still am a bit shocked," she said smiling as she slipped into her chair that was held out for her.

He waited for her to be seated and then he sat down.

They perused their menus and grew a bit silent.

"Well, thank you, and to make it up to you, I think we should order the champagne?" He suggested.

"Brilliant suggestion," she said. "Why be dampened by what went on? We should lighten the mood."

He smiled because he always knew they were on the same page. They ordered their drinks. He felt his coat pocket, and it was still there. He thought he would wait until after the main course.

"So, what are you having?" he asked slyly.

"Oh, it all looks so good. Perhaps the lobster. I mean, it goes well with the drinks." Kascey felt as if she was overindulging, and he was encouraging her.

"Great, so will I. I hear that it is the best."

She knew that something was up and figured that he had taken a hard hit at work. "Thank you. It is the first time in a while that we have had the same thing. Are events any better at work?"

"Yes, we have a new offering that we are working on. The other one has fallen and we cut our losses, and we are over it," he reassured her.

"Are you over it?" She inquired.

"Yes, I think so—and thank you for being so understanding and so supportive through it all. Thank you for being so supportive in general. These last few months have been magical. I really mean it."

"Oh, you are very welcome. You have been there for me also. Thank you," she replied. She really could not think of what had gotten over him.

"I would not have had it any other way. It has been my honor to be there for you," he said as they brought the courses. *So fast* he thought to himself. The service was so good that the waiters were on time with everything. He felt a surge of nerves, and his heart pounded. He knew the time had approached.

Therefore, he rummaged for something in his pocket and came around the table to her as if he had fallen and knelt. She looked at him shocked because she thought that he had dropped something or she had dropped something.

When he looked up at her, he said, "Will you marry me?" He pulled out the box and opened it.

It was a moment when her life flashed before her eyes and changed pages, and she was in a daze, astonished and searching for words. It was a beginning for them, and she felt transformed into a new woman in an instant. Her goals had been set with the right person, and she could not let him keep kneeling any more, she said, "Yes."

"Yes, I will marry you!" she exclaimed and then they heard an applause.

He got up, and they embraced. "Thank you, thank you," he said. He sat with a bit of a cramp in his knee as he fell hard on it at first.

"Congratulations!" could be heard coming from the tables closer to them but they could not hear it.

They delved further into each other's eyes and expressions.

"I love the ring," she commented admiringly as she watched it dazzle on her finger which was finally bejeweled. "I think it is beautiful and it is so sophisticated."

"Thank you. I got it on Saturday after I saw your parents. I just wanted you to like it."

"It is gorgeous," she continued. She could not stop looking at it glisten in the lighting.

The two finished their meal and ordered the white chocolate mousse cake to celebrate. They shared it as she savored each bite.

Grady was reassured that it had all happened as he had hoped and could not wait to text his parents, Kelly and Damien the code word: *Checkmate.* His parents were waiting eagerly for the code and perhaps he should, but he could not be distracted from the moment. The violinist came closer and played a favorite romantic tune as they glanced at each other a bit timidly. This was something that would take getting used to.

Kascey's mind wandered to the idea of an outdoor wedding with white linens and pale blues. They had more to discuss, and the day would soon come when she would be Kascey Kann Chisholm.

Grady was hoping for a quick engagement and a holiday wedding. He did not know if they could pull it off, and he did not want to rush it.

The evening dwindled to what seemed as just them and no one else in the restaurant. Nothing else existed for them at that particular moment.

After sipping coffee, they rose as he helped her with her chair and they strode out arm in arm. It was a beautiful evening, and the weather was mild in spring. The weather made the evening mystical; even the aroma from the pavements, as they strolled arm in arm seemed sweet. His comforting arms wrapped around her and sheltered her from the crisp air as they caught a taxi.

* * *

Kascey awoke still in euphoria. She felt more complete and with a compassed destiny. It was remarkable, and she could not believe that he had completely surprised her, and most of all, her parents knew and had kept the secret. The sun was nearing the center as busy bodies in the streets below scurried to their destinations. Her world had sat still. She made a cappuccino and sat on the settee and sipped it. Her world felt more connected to his.

Grady had gone to work and had informed his family about the good news.

Kascey called Ethan and Mabel and said, "I have great news!"

"Yes, dear, what is it?" Mabel had an inkling but did not want to say.

"Well! Grady proposed to me last night! Can you believe it?" she exclaimed.

"Yes, I sure can. That is great news. I wish you all the very best, dear," she replied relieved.

"Thank you, and you are not that surprised are you?" Kascey picked up on her mother's nonchalance.

"No, not really because he asked your father's blessing last week," Mabel admitted.

"Really, he did?" She asked startled.

"Yes, and we are so happy for you. Your father has gone to the shops, but I will tell him to call you as soon as he gets back. So when do you think the wedding will be?"

"Probably over the holiday season. I quite fancy an outdoor wedding. What do you think?"

Mabel was pleased to be included in at least the initial stages of the wedding. "Why, that sounds wonderful. It would have to be somewhere warm, of course."

"Yes, probably where we had our family vacations," Kascey suggested.

"Yes, that would be fine. Somewhere tropical," Mabel concurred.

"I will get back to you. How is the spring season coming along at the factory?"

"Very well, thank you. Our clothing is selling all over the world now—even in the South Pacific."

"Fabulous."

"I am doing my sketches, and we are hoping to get something going by the fall for me." She responded almost convincing herself.

"Well good luck. I know you can do it. You have designing in your genes. Remember that your family kept this community in fashion for a very long time."

"Yes, I know that. It is the fabric from whence I have come," she added sarcastically.

"That is right, and we are here to support you, dear. You know that," Mabel encouraged her. She was very supportive as most parents would feel as though they had completed their support by this time. Moda was completely on her own and Vasquez did not have that privilege when he was starting out. Kascey learned a lot about survival from them and was very thankful.

"Thank you so much, Mum. I look forward to hearing from Dad."

"Yes, you are very welcome. It was nothing, dear." Mabel hung up completely elated and bursting to tell her husband as soon as he walked through the door.

Kascey could not wait to tell her friends. Nathalie was coming over in a few hours and would be the third to know. On Monday, she would inform her boss and her colleagues all of whom admired Grady. Meanwhile, Grady had already headed back to work and was now working on an IPO for a communications company.

Chapter 13
CAPE'S HORN

In May, they spent a lovely late spring weekend in Cape Cod. The beach spanned for miles, and sleepy beach homes nestled along the shoreline. Grady's family summer house was one of them. *Silent Manor* was nestled along the roadside leading to the waterfront and was a washy blue beach villa with four bedrooms and a lovely veranda.

Lucinda was also arriving with her friend Trudy while Grady invited his college friend, Caleb K. Rolleys. Caleb was a venture capitalist and Grady thought it would be a good idea to go over ideas for Kascey's new business venture and to plan the wedding. Lucinda and Caleb would be standing in.

Kascey and Grady drove up to *Silent Manor*. It was welcoming as one could hear the small washes of the waves in the distance. They dragged their belongings to the veranda and opened the door. It was a cozy beach house with lovely wicker furniture and a large open kitchen that had been fully stocked by the weekend housekeeper. Jane loved living in the town and had been with the family since the seventies. She had stocked the freezer with Grady's favorite protein and candy bars from childhood and fruit and vegetables for the health-conscious fashionistas. Jane had a very close relationship with Kelly and acted as her eyes and ears.

Kelly and Damien were expecting to see the couple in a few weeks and would let the younger crowd enjoy their spring weekend at the Cape.

Kascey hoped to be inspired by the culture and the style for her spring collection. She thought of pastels and prints with sweeping styles.

Grady needed a break from the fiasco with Jacob Commerciale, which was almost the subject of a French stock investigation. It was new to him, and his office was complying fully with the requests. Luckily, he was able to save his career with the new communications offering.

"Oh, it is so divine. I really love this place. It reminds me so much of my beach vacations as a little girl," commented Kascey.

"Yes, it is like a second home for me. Caleb and I have spent many weekends here in our lifetime. We have this in common, and I hope we will be able to raise our family in this same villa."

"Yes, that would be lovely." Kascey looked around and got accustomed to it. She sat and took it all in as he rummaged around to find everything. "It is so peaceful and so calm here. I can hear the ocean." Kascey breathed in relief and was excited for the afternoon.

It was a Saturday morning and they would be taking the boat out when the others arrived. Grady was a skilled boater and longed to be on his vessel.

They heard a car. It was Lucinda and Trudy arriving in a hired car. They had taken a flight in and took a car from the airport. It was a good drive but had started early.

The doors shut, and the driver helped them with their luggage to the steps of the veranda.

Grady came out to assist. "Hello. Great that you made it on time," he remarked.

"Yes, we did. It was a beautiful drive over and such a gorgeous day," Lucinda answered pleased to see him.

"Hi Grady, how are you?" greeted Trudy.

"Fine, just fine —and happy to see you both. Kascey is just in the living room." He picked up the bags as Lucinda paid the driver.

Kascey stood by the door and waited to see Lucinda who had been a blessing for the business with all of her buying. They were all looking forward to the weekend together. Lucinda wore a large floppy brown hat and a linen summer dress while Trudy wore a bougainvillea plum summer dress and sandals. Trudy had been her friend from college in New Hampshire, and they had discovered New York together. Trudy once had an incessant crush on Grady and was reticent about the trip.

"Hello. It is so good to see you all again," Kascey greeted warmly.

"Yes, it is good to see you too. It is so nice to be at the villa again. It reminds me of old times," replied Lucinda.

"Hello, Kascey. How are you?" asked Trudy as she hobbled in with her overnight.

"Very well, thanks," replied Kascey.

"Great to hear. I am looking forward to the boat trip later this afternoon," stated Trudy.

"Yes, Grady is pretty excited about it. We are still waiting for one more," responded Kascey.

"Oh, has Caleb not arrived?" asked Lucinda. She also knew him from college when she would visit her brother.

"No, not yet," interjected Grady. "I think he said that his train arrives at noon so we still have a while before that. Well, we have not decided on the rooms, so you ladies choose first," offered Grady.

"Sure, shall we take a wander? I just love this house!" said Trudy.

They were expecting one more who was new to the group. Ray was a colleague of Caleb's and so there would be six.

The group fixed a lovely crab and lettuce salad, and Jane made some ranch dressing.

"I cannot believe this salad. Jane cooks so well," commented Trudy.

"Yes, this dressing is unbelievable. It is so smooth and creamy," remarked Kascey.

"I know. Jane can really cook. You should try her baked crab cakes. They are the best," Lucinda informed.

"So, Kascey, how is work in the fashion industry?" asked Trudy.

"It is fine. We are preparing for the winter collection now," stated Kascey not revealing too much. However, it was already rumored amongst them that she would be leaving.

"I see, and are you going on any more shows?" Trudy asked.

"I hope so. However, not right now," she answered a bit short.

Trudy looked at Lucinda a bit bewildered by the abrupt answer. Lucinda tried to suggest with her eyes to not ask any more questions.

Trudy complied and started on Grady. "So Grady, do you know much about Ray?"

"No, not really. He seems like a really cool guy, though. I mean, he has a good job and is from Connecticut. Basically, that is all I know."

"Oh, I see. Well, we are looking forward to meeting him." Trudy was hopeful now that Grady was no longer on the market.

"So, have you decided on a date and a location for the wedding?" inquired Lucinda excitedly.

"Yes. We think that it will be the week before the holidays in The Bahamas. Isn't that right dear?" he asked as he motioned toward Kascey.

"Yes, that is right. We will keep you posted. I have such fond memories on holiday there, and it is so convenient to fly for everyone. However, we will have to book fast because it is crowded at that time of year," continued Kascey.

"Oh, that sounds really wonderful. I cannot wait!" Lucinda exclaimed.

"I think the bridesmaids will wear a satin sea blue," considered Kascey.

"How amazing!" announced Lucinda as she turned her petite figure toward Trudy who nodded in agreement.

The group heard a car pull up, and it was Caleb and Ray. Grady could see Caleb's head and his aviation shades through the front window. Ray was athletically built and suited the role of a venture capitalist from New England with his confident appearance.

Trudy peered slightly mesmerized by his physique. Meanwhile, Lucinda was overjoyed by Caleb's arrival. They had a very amicable relationship.

"Great. They are here. Now we can go out on the boat," commented Grady as he walked outside to meet them. "Hey, welcome. How was your journey?"

"It was all right, man. You remember Ray, right?" asked Caleb.

"Yes, I remember from the last time. How are you doing? Thanks for coming down."

"My pleasure. Thanks for having me," Ray replied appreciatively.

"Come inside and meet my fiancée, my sister, and her friend."

"Sure thing," replied Ray.

The men climbed the stairs up to the veranda of the villa and entered the door.

"Hello, ladies," stated Caleb as he put his bags in the foyer.

"Hi, how are you? Glad that you made it up," replied Lucinda.

"Yes, good to see you," Kascey replied as Trudy gave him a brief hug.

"Have you met my friend Ray?" He introduced him as Ray greeted the ladies with a handshake.

"Nice to meet you," he said as he nodded.

"Okay," continued Caleb. "This is Kascey, Grady's fiancée, his sister Lucinda, and her friend Trudy."

"Hello," Kascey responded.

"Hi, nice to meet you," chimed Lucinda while Trudy expressed an "Enchanté," and extended her arm. He took it kindly in acknowledgement.

He said, "Fabulous! It is great to meet you."

"Now let's see which rooms you would like. Come this way," directed Grady who helped the guests settle in while the others finished lunch.

The group walked to the marina where Grady's vessel *The Harpoon* was parked. It was a Boston whaler that could easily fit six people. The men carried the coolers and packed snacks while the ladies brought aboard their necessities.

Grady took the steering wheel with ease and cautiously veered past the harbor and onto the open water. It was a calm day with a slight breeze and a low current. They sailed along the shoreline until maneuvering out to the ocean. The ladies waved to the people on the beach as they passed. Kascey and Lucinda stayed near the back of the boat and applied sunscreen. Trudy wandered to the front to chat with Caleb and Ray who were admiring the scenery.

The hull of the boat seared through the water as Grady picked up speed.

"Wow, this thing still has power!" he exclaimed to his mates.

"Yes, I see. Only a skilled boater could handle it," remarked Caleb.

"Well that I am!" boasted Grady. It was so serene to him, and his work issues were now miles away. Most importantly, he had found a funder for Kascey Kann Couture.

Trudy was admiring Ray and decided to join in the conversation. "So, Ray do you get to do a lot of boating?"

"Yes, reasonably. I have spent many summers on the sound and still get some down time there," he replied.

"Excellent. Do you have relatives or friends there?"

"Yes, I have a brother and his wife—also some friends from high school," he responded succinctly.

"I see. I go every Labor Day. Perhaps you can let me know when next you are down there," she suggested.

"Sure. That would be great!" he sounded optimistic and turned to look toward the hull as they glided on the water. Grady went further and further afield and was comfortable in the area.

"What do you think about Caleb?" Lucinda asked Kascey relishing her opinion.

"Ah, I think that he is a nice guy. I have only met him a few times, but from what I can see, I presume that you have known him a bit longer. Am I right?" Kascey asked inquisitively.

"Yes, I met him when I would visit Grady in New Hampshire. They were studying business together. He was also like a family member because they were so inseparable at the weekends when we were in college," explained Lucinda.

"Do I detect a bit of admiration?" asked Kascey.

"Probably—that is just what it is. That is why I am asking," Lucinda admitted.

"I see, well, yes—if you put it that way. I think that he is a nice guy. Has he asked you out?" Kascey pried.

"Not in so many words. I think that he will work up the nerve someday, but you know who is in the way. So, perhaps if you can distract Grady a bit, that would be fine," Lucinda suggested with a cunning look.

"Sure, you do not have to ask. Can you believe that we will be like sisters in a few months?"

"I know, my gosh. You have so much to do before the wedding. Let me know if I can be of any help. We have some fantastic dresses in for the spring, and they would be perfect, not only because I will be in the wedding but you should take a look," advised Lucinda.

"Sure, thanks. That would be perfect," responded Kascey appreciatively.

"How about you? I hear that you are transitioning soon. Is that something that scares you?" Pried Lucinda.

"No, not at all. I have been waiting my whole life for this. Really I have my own ideas now—something a bit more playful. I can envision lots of bolds and florals for the spring collection, and I want to do it." Kascey was absolutely confident about her new venture.

Lucinda looked around and did not recognize the waters. She felt a bit far out.

She called to Grady, "Grady, where are we?"

"I guess, just about eight knots west of the peak, I'd say."

"No, we look a bit farther. Are you sure?" she pressed speculating.

"Yes, I am pretty sure. Look at the navigator yourself." Grady looked down at the navigator and noticed that it had not moved for the last ten minutes and from that he guessed that it had not moved for a while before that. He tried not to panic, but he knew that they were lost. "Caleb, can you get over here?" he called out to him.

"Yes, what is it?"

"This navigator has not moved. Try your phone and see if you can get a signal. We are off course," he cautioned.

"What? Okay." Caleb tried to get a signal, but they were too far from the shoreline.

Grady looked around to see if he could decipher where they were. He hoped that they had not made it to Nantucket or Maine. He knew that he was out in open waters and decided to turn off the boat and anchor. He pressed the alarm button and hoped it would be sensed.

It was already four and the afternoon sun had left its highest peak and was dwindling. Soon it would be dark.

Grady called for Kascey, "Kascey, have you got your iPad on you?"

"Sure, but I do not know if it can work. Why?"

"We have to get a message out. Sorry, guys. I have no clue where I am. The navigator was broken. I am off the chart. We have to call for help," he said commiserating.

Kascey became worried because she had never seen Grady like that. "I hope that it will work, dear. I will try to get all of the messaging on. Who do you want to message?"

"Message the coast guard. I'll give you the address and my Dad, Damien. He should know where we are," demanded Grady agitated.

"Gosh, we just got this thing fixed. I cannot believe it."

"No worries, man. Things will be fine. I will check my phone and send a text. That should work."

The group waited over an hour before they received help. It was difficult for him to describe where he had ventured. They were relieved when they saw the coast guard who led them safely back to shore.

Kascey, Lucinda, and Trudy huddled at the back of the boat while Ray stood by in a more comforting role. It had been a long afternoon and Kascey was ready to get back to shore and prepare the barbecue for the evening. She looked at the falling sun of the cape as it was almost six when they arrived back.

They disembarked and thanked the coast guard. They all jumped in the jeep with their belongings and drove back to villa.

"I am exhausted. I cannot believe the long day," commented Trudy.

"Yes, I think I'll rest up before dinner. I am a bit tired," said Lucinda.

"Sounds good. What time do you want to prepare dinner?" asked Grady.

"At around eight. We can just hang out on the veranda and grill the lobster and crab," responded Lucinda. She was accustomed to the lazy summer evenings at the Cape with her family and friends and was looking forward to the down time. Jane would be over in the morning, and then they would head back to the city on Sunday night. Jane helped Kelly keep tabs on her children's lives.

Grady sat next to Kascey on the settee and whispered, "That really freaked me out today."

"I know. Do not worry. It all went well—and we are back safely," she reassured him.

"I know. I realized how important you are to me. What would have happened if I would have lost everything?"

"Not to worry because it did not happen," she continued.

"Thanks for being so understanding. What would I do without you?" Grady knew that he had a rock of Gibraltar with Kascey.

* * *

Lucinda arose looking well rested and wandered to the kitchen where she found Caleb and Grady collecting the seafood for the grill.

"Oh, hello, I can help. Let me make the salad and wash the potatoes for you," she offered.

"Great. Jane bought some vegetables for the salad, and I think that the potatoes are in the compartment," replied Grady appreciatively.

"That's okay. I will look for everything. I see that Kascey has already got the plates and utensils out," she commented.

"Yes, she lent a helping hand."

"Fabulous. I will just do my thing," continued Lucinda who was accustomed to her bit over dinner. She did not want to leave a mess for Jane or else Kelly would find out.

"Please let me know if you need any more help?" offered Kascey.

"Oh, I am fine—just relax. Trudy and Ray should be around somewhere," commented

Lucinda as she looked around for her friend who was noticeably not there. She glanced at Ray on the veranda helping out with the refreshments.

"I cannot believe this lobster, look at it!" remarked Grady.

"Yes, it is large and perfect!" commented Ray.

"Look at that," Grady said.

The men started to talk about their latest work projects. Ray boasted about his new IPO while Caleb spoke about his latest venture. Grady boasted about the communications IPO, which was a success, and tried to brush the Jacob Commerciale ordeal under the carpet. He and Claude had washed their hands of it a few weeks back and hopefully for good.

Lucinda walked out and placed the salad on the buffet table while handing the potatoes to Caleb to grill. Trudy and Lucinda followed with the glasses and some more ice from the freezer.

"Okay, everyone. Just grab what you want and take a seat. No particular order," offered Grady.

The lounge chairs were strategically placed in little groups around the porch, which was lit by the hanging lanterns.

"It is one beautiful night, isn't it, Kascey?" observed Grady as they both sat and started to bite into their food.

"I know. It is perfect—just perfect. I cannot believe how lovely it is out here this time of the year. I wish it would last."

She did and it was a beautiful moment as they all laughed and tucked into their dinner. They must have spent the entire evening outside watching the stars and the boats go by. They laughed and talked until well after midnight, and by that point, had throws and pashminas to protect them from the sea's cool breeze.

Chapter 14
CALM SUNDAY

The group nestled about the villa and had not made it to their rooms after a long night of talking. It was already ten, and Jane arrived to meet them all getting up. The sun had risen and warmed the interior through the windows.

Lucinda was up early and had dressed because Jane was expected. On her cue, the others headed to get ready for the day.

Jane arrived promptly and started the washing up. She was to make her famous banana and rose petal pancakes for brunch with lovely cranberry seltzer and poached eggs. She knew it was Lucinda's favorite.

"Hello there. It is so nice to see you again," Lucinda greeted Jane. "I am so sorry about the mess, but we hung out all night and we just got up," she explained.

"Hello to you too. That is fine. It makes it feel like old times," commented Jane who had been there for numerous mornings.

"You are such a sport. Thanks. Now, there are six of us. That's right. Can you believe it?"

"All right. I will make enough and pour some more coffee for you all. Where will you sit? In the dining room? Let's make it fancy. So, is the soon-to-be Mrs. here as well?"

"Yes. We all got in yesterday, and the wedding will be in Bimini. I will keep you posted," informed Lucinda.

"Ah, very nice. I cannot wait," she replied.

Jane started in the kitchen while she picked up and folded the throws and the cushions. She could smell the fresh cleaner from as a child, and it brought back memories of days gone by on the Cape.

"Have you heard from your mother?" asked Jane.

"Yes. She called yesterday to see if we were okay. We all got lost on the boat."

Jane had heard about the boat incident in town and was rest assured that they all got back safely.

At that moment, Grady appeared when he smelled the aromas from the kitchen.

"Jane, hello it is so nice to see you," he said as he gave her a hug.

"Great to you see you, my boy." The two had a special relationship and she considered him to be a second son.

"Thanks for coming over to make brunch. I really appreciate it." He was always concerned for her.

"It is my pleasure. Is the new family member up yet?" asked Jane.

Grady laughed. "Yes, she is almost ready and she will be out soon."

The rest of the group sauntered out one by one and sat around until brunch was ready. The men were planning to take a jog on the beach after brunch while the ladies decided to go to town to do some shopping. Lucinda and Kascey were curious about the latest town fashions. Kascey wanted to get some ideas for her spring look. This was a niche which was worth targeting.

Kascey entered the room looking surprisingly spritely for five or six hours' sleep.

"Morning, everyone. How are you, Jane?" she asked as they were very cordial.

"Fine, thanks, Miss Kann—and congratulations to you! We are all so excited to hear your big news. Now Luce has been filling me in, but do tell," persisted Jane.

"Thank you. I am very excited. Look!" Kascey extended her finger toward Jane who took a long look.

"Why that is absolutely lovely. I cannot believe Grady is getting married."

"Yes, you will hear about the plans as we get them. We hope that you can attend," reassured Kascey.

"Oh, thank you and that would be very nice," replied Jane proudly.

Jane had a very nurturing aspect about her and was more than just the house keeper to the family. She had confided in Kelly for many years of their upbringing and had become a member of the family.

"It all smells so good on Sundays," commented Kascey.

"Thanks, dear. Now have a seat, and I will be right over with the food," stated Jane.

The crew sat at the table while brunch was being served.

Caleb and Ray could not believe how incredible it all smelled. Grady tucked into her meal while the ladies were a bit more polite and cautious around the men.

"Wow, this is delicious Jane," complimented Caleb as she came in with more coffee.

"Thank you, Jane. This is lovely," added Trudy and savoring each mouthful.

"Well I have not had a meal like this in ages," commented Ray.

"Thank you dears, and it is my pleasure— now eat up," Jane said.

She knew that they were a good crew of children, and to her they will always be. She had memories of summers with the family and friends, Kelly and Damien's dinner parties with the neighbors and business associates. It was her duty to hold the family together and she took her job very seriously as a loyal friend.

* * *

After a long afternoon and fabulous outdoor outings, they took a van to be dropped off at their particular modes of transport. Kascey had a brilliant weekend and felt rejuvenated for the coming week. It was what she needed to keep her mind off her transition. Grady was refreshed, and he felt as though he could conquer his issues at work. Trudy felt as if she had found a special new friend in Ray with whom she had exchanged details. Lucinda on the other hand, was still not sure where she stood with Caleb. However, she knew that eventually it would be determined.

Chapter 15

NORMAL DAYS

The summer had begun and New York began to swelter as June's glow reigned. Grady had an eventful Friday dealing with his next IPO. He had plans in motion with Caleb to fund Kascey's new venture. They had determined that an initial capital outlay of $8 million would suffice for a small operation. This amount had the potential to grow over a number of years as the business grew. He knew Kascey had the stamina to see the business succeed.

His parents were staying at an upscale hotel near the park. They were going to have dinner with Kascey and him in a few hours. Once they had arrived and were checked in, they decided to spend the afternoon walking along the park and shopping. Kelly wanted to take advantage of the sales before dinner. She and Damien strolled in familiar territory where they would shop for the children when they were smaller and enjoyed the walk down memory lane.

"My, isn't it a glorious afternoon?" remarked Kelly.

"Yes, it surely is. It is nice to have a break in the city," commented Damien.

"Certainly. Now let's go in this store. I really want to get something for the summer in the Cape." The family had been spending the summer there for decades; it was close to where she grew up with her family.

They entered the store as the cold air overcame them in a refreshing way. It was almost frigid in comparison to the hot June outside. Kelly was in wonderland as she browsed and picked up items for the summer.

"Okay, you shop while I'll wait here," suggested Damien.

"Sure. I won't be too long," she replied.

He took a seat and unwrapped a newspaper.

Kelly tried on her outfits and decided to purchase five. She called him over with the cards.

"Okay, dear. Which one should I use?" he asked.

"I guess the platinum," he diligently pulled them from his wallet and chose which one while handing it to the cashier.

"Thank you, sir" she responded courteously.

When they were done, they left the store and took another stroll on the east side of Manhattan.

"Do you remember the old surrey rides?" she asked.

"Yes, like yesterday." He replied smiling.

"Yesterday," she replied. She remembered the aroma of the sweet candy on the street being warmed by the vendors. The whole area had the aroma and the children were delighted. There were many visits without them when they would go to the theater and have skyline dinners. The memories were abundant.

Kelly was excited to have dinner with her soon to be daughter-in-law. It was such a thrill to get to know the next Mrs. Chisholm. She was very protective of her children and knew that Grady was in good hands. Kascey was a sturdy and headstrong young lady who had the ability to cope with any situation and she knew that her characteristics were soon to be tested.

By evening, the couple headed back to the hotel where they readied for the occasion.

Kelly had chosen an authentic steakhouse near the park with tablecloths and chandeliers. Kascey dressed to impress her soon to be in-laws with a conservative top and fitted skirt. She and Grady arrived together and greeted his parents who were waiting at the bar sipping refreshing drinks after a humid June day.

"Hello, dear," Kelly greeted her son affectionately. He was excited to see them after a few months.

"Hello, Mom. Hello, Dad. How have you been?" He had not had a chance to talk to them since they arrived.

"Fantastic—and we are sure happy to be here," she replied as she kissed her son on the cheek and greeted Kascey.

"Dad, good to see you," he remarked as he shook his father's hand.

"Son, it's great to see you too—and congratulations on the news!"

"Kascey, congratulations, dear," interrupted Kelly as she looked at her warmly. "How was the Cape?"

"It was great. Thank you for letting us stay. I am so happy and the Cape was as fabulous as ever. The group had a wonderful time, and it was so nice to see Lucinda and Jane again."

"Splendid. I heard that it went well," responded Kelly.

"Yes, except for the boat issue, which is now fixed. They surely do not make them like they used to," admitted Damien.

"No. They do not. It was such a harrowing experience, Dad," replied Grady.

"Yes, we were quite frightened until the coast guard arrived," commented Kascey. "We did not know what to do, but Grady handled it perfectly."

"Sure, he is an experienced boater," complimented his father who smiled at his son.

When they were seated, Kelly and Kascey chatted about her new move and her wedding.

"I am really excited to go to Bimini for the wedding. Thank you for having it before the holidays so we can get home to the family," started Kelly who was bursting with excitement.

"So am I. I have four bridesmaids, and Grady has four groomsmen. We are hoping to invite about fifty guests, and everyone is so excited.

They cannot wait for the invites, and the wedding is a whole six months away."

"I know. Well, I would really appreciate it if you could invite Grady's Godmother, Sylva, and my sister Mavey. They will never forgive me if they do not go."

"Sure. I think that they are already included," reassured Kascey.

"Also, my first cousin on my mother's side who moved back to Ireland, Nancy."

"Yes. I think that Grady has mentioned her," continued Kascey.

"Good. She is an author and does travel writing for a large network," said Kelly.

"Oh, that should be very interesting. I come from a small family, but there are some family friends I should invite as well and also my colleagues from work."

"Now, do tell me how that is going?" Kelly pried.

"It is going quite well. I have not handed in my official notice yet. I will soon, very soon. Grady has already helped me to get the wheels in motion for my transition."

"Nice. Good luck. I know that you will do well."

"Thanks. I really appreciate that," responded Kascey.

The couples gave their orders and talked about the future. Damien was concerned about his son's involvement with Jacob Commerciale and needed to see if the investigation had cleared. Grady reassured him that it had and that they had complied with any investigation in Europe.

"There is nothing to worry about. Trust me. We have complied with the investigations and it is now up to the jurisdiction," he reassured his father.

"That is good to hear because we were very worried. The industry has changed immensely since I retired several years back. I just want you to know that you have my support if you need it," Damien reassured him.

"Thank you. I appreciate it. It is just a simple cross-border administration issue that can be ironed out in no time. It would have not been an issue had the initial public offering performed as it should have," Grady continued.

"I know—and that is what I wish to tell you. It will not go the way envisioned all the time and one has to remember to ask all the questions and to be thorough —or else you will get what happened in this situation, and that is people on your case. I know it is not your fault." Damien was definite in his advice to his son as there was no room for error in this financial environment.

"Thanks, Dad. Thank you for looking out for me," Grady responded bravely to his father's advice.

Kascey and Kelly were still embroiled in a discussion over the wedding plans and he was chuffed at how happy they looked. He knew that it was the beginning of happier times together as a family.

After dinner, they walked back to the hotel. Kascey and Grady bid farewell for the evening and took a taxi downtown. The weather was mild for the beginning of summer. There was so much to plan and to fit in all for their trips. They had hoped for a summer trip to Monaco by Labor Day.

More importantly, Kascey had to break the news to Vasquez that she was leaving to start her new project. It was a difficult time for him, and the news would be devastating.

Damien and Kelly still had another day in the city and decided to go to the theater before meeting the new couple for dinner again. This time Lucinda would join them and was bringing a new date, Nate, whom she had met at a retail conference. He works as the chief executive of a rival department store in Connecticut.

They all met at a trendy restaurant in the Flatiron District that had silk white table- cloths and red stems hanging from the ceiling.

Nate was a bundle of nerves. Kascey took pity on him because she remembered that it was not long ago when she was in the hot seat. He shyly shook everyone's hands as she introduced him to her family.

Grady looked him square in the face. "I am very pleased to meet you. I hear that you hail from Connecticut?"

"Yes, that is right. Stamford to be exact." He was relieved that someone broke the ice for him.

"Yes. I have been there. Great town," Grady replied.

"I know it as well," Damien added. "I had a big client from there for many years."

"I see. My folks are still there, and I work a few towns over," he continued.

"Hello. I am Kelly," she interrupted keenly.

"Hello, Mrs. Chisholm. It is so nice to meet you. I have heard so much about you from Lucinda," he responded politely.

"It is my pleasure, Nate. I am thrilled that you could join us," she replied amicably.

"Oh and this is Kascey, Grady's fiancé," Lucinda revealed.

"Hello, the pleasure is also mine," she said as she extended her hand to meet his.

The group perused the menus quietly.

"My, what a lovely place, Lucinda. It looks so interesting," her mother remarked.

"Thank you. I have been here once or twice with colleagues, and I thought that it would be a good place to meet," she responded.

They placed their orders and continued to chat.

Damien thought that he would pry a bit more. "So, Nate, how is the retail business?"

"It is picking up thankfully," he responded optimistically. "I have an MBA degree and decided there was an area in the business in my home state. Most people choose between there and the city to shop, and I saw the perfect opportunity. I must say there was worry in the industry for a while, but there have been improvements in sales.

We are looking forward to a rewarding holiday season."

"Finally! A bit of good news, and I could not agree with you more," enthused Damien.

"That's right. I have seen more interest in this industry in the past few months. Especially in the middle-end retail—less in specialty—hence Kascey's decision to branch out on her own," remarked Grady.

Kascey overheard her name but became interested in the conversation between the women of the group on the side.

"Mom, what do you think?" Lucinda whispered.

She looked at her daughter and lowered her voice. "He is a very nice young man. So charming and respectful. Oh yes. I think that he is a keeper," she uttered teasing and still not wanting to give an approval so soon without knowing him.

"Okay, and you, Kascey?"

She did not want to be overheard since the conversation had calmed down between the men. "Fabulous, a very nice person. Will we be seeing more of him?" she inquired.

"I hope so. We get on so well, and I have known him almost a month."

Kascey had not seen her this happy. She was not this happy around Caleb whom she thought would have been the one. She felt a sense of regret. *Poor Caleb. Did he know? Did he care?* It was all moving a bit too fast for Kascey to comprehend.

"So Nate, do you like boating?" asked Kelly.

"Yes, very much. We spent the summers in Nantucket and had a schooner." He replied impressively.

"Oh, that is very nice. It is one of my most favorite places to visit. Well, we shall have to invite you to the Cape since you are familiar with the territory. Lucinda spent many summers there," explained Kelly.

"Yes, she has told me. I would like to very much—and thank you for the invitation," he responded politely and feeling more comfortable.

Kascey was silent over the conversation as she waited for it to unravel. She liked him for Lucinda and found him to be a very decent person. It was a contrast to Lucinda's sparkling personality.

"Yes, that would be superb. I can hardly wait!" exclaimed Lucinda.

Damien appeared to look at Kelly a bit askance because it was a rather soon to be handing out invites. However, he was sensitive about how happy it made Lucinda and chimed in with his approval.

Damien and Kelly had an early flight back. Kelly was saddened that she would have to wait until later in the summer—or even the fall—before she saw her children again. She had always been a very protective mother, and age made no exception to her rules. What was precious to her remained precious to her after all the years.

"Now remember, son, what we have discussed, and if you need any more advice, please come to me. I still have my connections in the industry and can help you in any situation," he reassured Grady.

"Thank you. I will remember that," he responded as he shook his hand and then hugged Kelly good-bye.

"Good luck, you two, with your wedding plans. Remember to call me if you need any help with the organizing," stated Kelly as she made her good-byes. The hardest being to her only daughter who had a beau with her.

"Bye Mom. Call you tomorrow and have a safe trip back," Lucinda said.

"Bye, dear. Thank you, and see you soon Kascey. Bye Nate. Lovely to see you and take care. See you again soon." Kelly waved as Damien hugged Lucinda and Kascey good- bye.

"Take care of yourselves. Bye now, and take care of her Nate," he said as he shook his hand.

"I will. Bye and thank you all for a lovely dinner. It was a pleasure meeting you all."

"Oh, the pleasure was ours. Bye. Bye Grady," Kelly remarked as she and Damien stepped into a cab. It was so hard leaving them again. She had made that scenario many times before. She waved as the taxi pulled off and the group of four remained on the sidewalk in the warmth of the summer breeze as the taxi sped toward midtown.

Chapter 16

NEW MONDAY

It was a sweltering day at the end of June. The wedding invites were due from the calligraphers to be sent to the invitees. Grady had floated another successful offering, and the new plans for the fashion house were almost operational. The day had optimism. Charlene was settled and working smoothly as their new designer, the marketing plan was a success, and they were taking many online prêt–à–porter orders.

Vasquez's winter collection was almost ready with Mari and Charlene adding the finishing touches. Kascey felt uneasy as she knew that this would be the day to give Vasquez her notice. There would be two months for him to find a suitable replacement, and she hoped they would not be too grueling.

She walked into the company which had the distinct Garment District Monday morning fragrance of cut fabrics and fresh cloth. Her styles were hanging on the mannequins as she gathered her shears and kit to start at the machine. Vasquez was on the phone with the marketing executives and very pleased with the online campaign that had recently begun. Kascey needed to speak to him and waited as she prodded the black fabric for the main dress at the Paris show.

He hung up cheerily and walked over to speak to her. "Hello, Kascey. That was marketing, and I have a few interviews approaching with some major networks about the new line. This has been a dream come true. It seems as if I am getting more attention from the lower end of the line than before." It was important for him to share the news with her.

"Fabulous. That is great news. When did they say they needed you?" she asked worried that it would be when she would be about to leave.

"In August. I still have a few more weeks to prepare. I have not done a proper interview in a few years on home territory. This is major," he boasted.

"Great. I am so happy that it is all working out for you. I told you that it would," she replied reassuringly.

Just then, Charlene passed by as cheerful as usual. They both waved.

"I am so pleased how it is working out with Charlene. Good choice, Kascey," thanked Vasquez whole heartedly.

"Oh, Vasquez, she is so talented. Really, we have found a gem in her. I think she will do superbly at the next shows," continued Kascey.

"We shall see. I mean the couture is not really her thing. That is for you," he responded loyally.

"Well, that is what I really need to discuss with you," Kascey replied woefully.

He felt a singe of the unknown and grew wary of her response, "What do you mean? Please do not say this to me, Kascey," he complained in response.

"So sorry," she responded tepidly, "It is true. I cannot stay any longer. We have had a long history, and I have learned a great deal, but surely with my entrepreneurial background, I am sure that you had an idea that one day I would have to branch out," she explained cautiously.

"Yes. I have, but I never thought that it would come at this moment. We are just trying to get things to turn around—and then there was the patent infringement and the theft before the show. Surely, you can see what we have been through. The company still needs you," he pleaded.

"No. You do not really need me anymore. You can do this. It is your name on the brand—not mine. Vasquez, this is your empire and I need to create my own ideas."

"No, no Kascey—not now. How will I replace you?" he said frantically.

"Well, I have given it some thought, and perhaps we will find someone. I can stay on until the end of August. We will finalize the show and do the interviews—and then I will have to start fresh for the fall."

"Thank you, then. I appreciate it." He knew that he could not have kept her for much longer. The last few years have been borrowed time and he knew that she had her own ideas and so much talent. "So, what type of line are you thinking?" He queried despondently.

"I want to do something a bit sportier—with some cocktail or party dresses. A bit more youthful for a different market," she explained awkwardly.

"I see. That should work. You have the talent. I am so very proud of you—regardless of what you choose."

He meant it, however, it was still a sudden blow to him—and to his image. At least her line would be different for now. He knew that he had trained her to be a master at a different line, and eventually she would miss her true form. He felt as if he had let her down and not offered her more, but it was still his line. He looked over at Charlene, and it all fell into place. Kascey had been thinking of it for a while, and the best he could do for her was to let her go and spread her wings. His was a world of creation, and the talent created by Kascey was no exception and should be cultivated.

* * *

Kascey was still a bit overcome by the conversation. She had to call Grady.

Grady was finishing up his orders with Norma when the phone rang. "Hello," he answered when he saw her number.

"Is this a bad time?" she asked.

He could tell by her rushed tone that it was urgent. "No, no, it's fine." He motioned for Norma to give him some time.

"Good. Well, I have had the discussion with Vasquez and have told him," she confessed.

"How did he take the news?" He probed.

"Not too well. It was very difficult, but we have come to the agreement that I will stay until August. He has interviews coming up," she continued.

"Well, do not worry. The worst is now over. He has to accept this okay. He will accept this. Just give him time." Grady always advised her on office issues and might have to think about a more active role in her company if he continued. "It will all go smoothly. I promise," he comforted her.

"Thank you. You are always so supportive. You need to be my partner. I'll call you later," she said rushing off the phone.

"Okay, but we can always discuss another manager at a later date," he replied jokingly. "Talk to you soon," and then he hung up.

It was true, Vasquez would move on and realize that he could find a replacement. No one was that indispensable, and there were many like

Kascey. He only needed to look. The afternoon became mundane, and soon it was time to leave for the day.

* * *

Kascey slumped on her couch and commiserated over how her day unraveled. She was looking forward to dinner when she heard a knock on the door.

It was Nathalie checking in on her, "Hello. I just thought that I would stop by. Is this a bad time? We got off work at a reasonable time tonight."

Kascey motioned for her to enter, and she sat on the sofa. "Thank you for stopping by. It is all right. Can I offer you a drink?"

"Sure. I will have whatever you have in the fridge. I understand that this is just an impromptu visit," Nathalie replied apologetically.

"Oh, that is fine. I could use a bit of cheering up. I gave my notice today. I feel horrible. I am branching off on my own," revealed Kascey.

"Really? That's great. Good luck," said Nathalie in surprise. "So have you where you are going to set up in mind?"

"Yes, I think somewhere in the Flatiron District closer to here. Also, Grady has been assisting with the planning. I just have to get a lease, and we will be all set," responded Kascey contemplating her next move.

"Fantastic. I mean, I do hope it all works out for you. Let me know if you need some friendly advice or motivation. I am always here. Remember that," Nathalie reassured her. She was always there and knew what it was like to pursue similar goals in the city and how necessary it was to have a kind soul to watch one's back.

"Thank you. I appreciate it." Kascey placed two homemade lemonades on the table. "I hope that this is okay. I am not drinking alcohol tonight because I have another busy day tomorrow. The new orders are flying off the wall."

"This is fine. Thank you." She accepted that Kascey could be a hard worker and was strict with her regime. "So, we have not caught up for a few weeks. How are Grady's parents? How did that all pan out?" Nathalie asked.

"It was fantastic. We had a splendid time. They are a fantastic set of people, and his sister brought her new date with her who is actually very nice. His name is Nate, and she is really into him I suppose," revealed Kascey.

"That is a relief, but regarding his sister, unbelievable, I mean, I thought that you were trying to set her up with Caleb remember?" She replied confused.

"Well, apparently, that is not the situation and she now has a boyfriend. So, that is all set in stone I suppose. As for his parents, they were as sweet as ever. I have really lucked out with that family. I wish that we could have spent more time. Grady is still stressed out about his work though, and I often worry about him," continued Kascey.

"I see, well that is understandable. He has such a highly pressurized job which involves deals all over the world." She changed the topic, "Now what about plans for the wedding? She continued very excited about the new prospect.

"Yes, we have a date set. It will be on December Twenty first—and then we all come back for the holidays. The honeymoon will be over New Year's eve just because it would be so selfish to avoid our families over the holidays," stated Kascey considerately.

"I know, and that makes it easier for the guests to return home for the holidays. That is so thoughtful, and it all sounds so lovely. Have you decided where you will live?" Nathalie was concerned because she was still worried about losing her favorite neighbor.

"Yes. I think that we will live downtown before we buy something." She frowned in response.

"Oh no. So, you will give up this bachelorette pad? I will have a new neighbor." Nathalie sighed and was extremely disappointed by the concept. She and Kascey had grown close and had shared so many aspirations over the time.

"Not for a little while. We can make the most of it before that comes. I just want to thank you for all the housesitting during my travels," Kascey reassured her knowing that the end was in sight.

"Not to worry about the housesitting. It was all fine by me—and it was never a problem. Now that you will not be with the company, will you have shows to attend?" She queried.

"Well, that is the hard part. They will be a different type of show before I can get more grounded and better known. I know. It is the hardest thing to realize that my life is going to be so different in a few months. I will have a new office, new staff, company credit, and then a new place." Kascey held her head in her hands almost in horror of the prospect of all of the changes.

"I know. "How will you manage? It seems as though you will go through many transitions."

"I know, but it will all be worth it. The good thing about it is that we will all get together for the wedding. Therefore, I will see my old friends from the office in Bimini and some will stand. Of course, I will need you to be my bridesmaid. I have chosen Moda as maid of honor and Lucinda as another bridesmaid. Grady has decided on Caleb as best man, and then his colleague, Claude will be a groomsman. It will be fantastic," Kascey explained. She was almost talking herself into getting over the long list of what she had to do.

"Oh. It all sounds fantastic," she replied. "How do your parents feel?"

"They are fine with all of it. They are excited about the wedding. They are excited about my new move and want to help with the manufacturing. I mean it is all thought out now. I can't wait for you to see them again. You will see them during the wedding," Kascey promised.

"I cannot wait. My, look at the time! I had better get going. I have a Skype appointment but thanks for the refreshing lemonade. We will catch up later," said Nathalie. "I will stop by later in the week."

"It was my pleasure. Come by anytime. You see, I feel much better. I had better change anyway because I am meeting Grady for dinner in an hour," replied Kascey.

"Great, you do that. See you again soon," responded Nathalie.

Kascey felt better. Hearing herself plan made her see the big picture of how the rest of the year was scheduled. And this reminded her that she had to call the wedding planner in Bimini in the morning to confirm the numbers. She dressed for dinner preferring a baby blue sun dress and sling backs for the occasion.

Dinner had a slight overcast because of events earlier that day. Kascey was still affected by her conversation with Vasquez and surprised by the way that he took her leaving. There was still so much ground to cover until then. When returned to her apartment, she noticed that she had missed a few phone calls from Moda and decided to call her before retiring for the evening.

* * *

After dinner, she called Moda. "I am sorry I have not called sooner. Grady and I had dinner close by, and my phone's ringer must have been turned off.

"I see. That is okay. I have been trying to reach you because I heard some rumors today and had to call you?" responded Moda rather inquisitively.

Kascey could not believe that it was out already, but it was a small company. "I guess you have heard that I am leaving, and yes it is true." She admitted.

"Really? Why? I cannot believe you did not tell me, your best friend," remarked Moda feeling sidelined.

"Sorry. I just could not tell anyone before letting Vasquez know. We will still have fabulous times, and you are my maid of honor. I will still need some modeling done," continued Kascey, "So. It is not like it is the end of the world or anything. I am just moving in a new direction, you will see," she reassured her.

"Really? You mean that you will stay in the business?" She responded relieved.

"Yes, of course I am. I really need to be on my own as I have so many ideas, and they are not in line with Vasquez. That is all. Listen you can come with me to find a new location," negotiated Kascey to soothe her excitement.

"Incredible. So you are not relocating out of the city? Just starting your own business?" Moda understood the situation a bit better, and felt slightly foolish and relieved.

"Yes, and I will design more activewear and casual wear. You will see. It will be completely different from what I am doing now."

"Oh. It sounds so exciting. I cannot wait to do some modeling for you, of course, if Vasquez will not mind. How did he take the news?" asked Moda.

"Not as I had hoped. In all honesty, he could have been a bit more polished, but that is to be expected I suppose. We have been through so much together. I hope that this will not jeopardize what we have achieved over the past years," added Kascey concerned.

"I know how you feel. I would not leave him right now, I mean, nothing to do with you. It is just that I still would like to cover more ground with him career wise," explained Moda.

"I understand. However, I still have time at the company over the next eight weeks. It should be fabulous," she responded.

"I know, but the shows will be so different without you," Moda felt the void already of the difference, and her heart slumped slightly that eight weeks would not be a very long time at all, and that after the summer, things would be different.

"Do not say that just yet. I do hope to attend some shows on my own you know." The truth about Kascey was that she was so talented that everyone was certain that her business would flourish. The ladies spoke more about the wedding and then signed off for the evening. Kascey was concerned about how she would face the day and hoped that Vasquez would take it better.

* * *

That evening, Vasquez embarked on a restless night as he thought of the stress of replacing Kascey, and how much they had gone through in the business. He and his family had just moved to the Hamptons for the summer, and he could hear the echo of the shoreline in the background. He decided that he needed to hire a designer from her school of thought and would look in Europe for the answer. There were enough budding designers who were ready to make their mark in the world, and he was willing to approach them. He looked over at his wife Daphne as she lay sleeping with no idea of what he was going through. He decided not to talk about it until he had found a solution. Vasquez had enough to think about regarding his empire to allow this obstacle to hold him back.

The evening was calm in late June as he peered out the window onto the lawn. The sun had already risen, and he put a fresh pot on to brew. He had a long day ahead, and he wanted to be ready. This summer would be different from the others which would be filled with charity galas and lazy afternoons on the tennis court. He was starting anew, and he needed to hustle to achieve his goals as he did when he started. He was confident because he had the right marketing team—and now, thanks to Kascey, he had a brilliant new team.

Chapter 17

HAZY DAYS OF SUMMER

It was already 6 p.m. and the last weekend in August had begun. It was a long weekend, and the mist from a sweltering day had started to lift in downtown NYC. Kascey wore a black spaghetti strap summer dress and wedged heels as she sipped an espresso at the corner shop in SoHo. She waited for her fiancé Grady to arrive. They were taking a long weekend the next morning to France and Monte Carlo for the end of the summer before starting their new projects.

Kascey's business was nearly underway. She had her Kascey Kann Couture license and had found her new location, a beautiful loft in the Flatiron District. She had her new technological system set up and had hired two assistants, Judy and Sire, to start in mid-September upon her return. Her business plan and the finding of venture capitalists had been solidified by Grady's strong business sense and efforts. Also, they had the task of viewing apartments on their return as a marital home in December. It was an option to moving in with him downtown. Her life had taken off at an exponential rate, and a lovely week in Monaco was what she needed to get on track.

She sipped her coffee as he entered the quaint shop and approached her seat.

"Hello, Kascey," he said as he greeted her with a kiss and a hug.

"Hi. What are you having?"

"I'll just get the usual. Have you been waiting here long?" he asked concerned.

"No, not too long. How was your day?"

"Fabulous. I have been on the phone to your funders and we are ready for the fifteenth—just as planned."

She grew excited and was filled with such hope that her new business was starting. "Thank you. I am so excited. I have the designs all ready, and Sire and Judy have already been in touch to start the manufacturing and production. We will be right on target," she responded confidently.

"That's good. It sounds promising to hear. Now, our flight is in the morning. We will have a week in Monaco to do whatever you want. I really want to relax and tour the area. We have earned this vacation," he asserted.

"I know. I just want to visit it without any stress. I know that I will miss everyone. By the way, they are having a going-away party for me when I get back just before I start my business. Please say that you will come?"

"Yes, of course, but let us think more about where we are," he continued as he sipped his Frappuccino. "We have to send out the invites for the wedding when we get back. Also, we must look at apartments. I so very much would like you to move downtown, but if you are looking for something more residential. Then, we should think about the Upper East Side or Gramercy?"

"Of course. I will contact the wedding planner when we return to see where we are regarding that," she said agreeing. She would need more space to start a family with him and wanted a more convenient location to get to her studio and the children's schools. "I am all packed and ready for the flight. What do you want for dinner? It is already seven o'clock."

"Oh, something light. We have a long flight in the morning and I cannot wait to splurge when we arrive." He always cherished his European adventures with her, and this was a special trip as singletons before they were betrothed. They settled on grilled shrimp Caesar salads for dinner and espressos before calling it a night.

Kascey had a rather tumultuous night in her apartment full of uncertainty. She had so much to think about and had left a list for Nathalie. Nathalie, Moda and Lucinda were standing in the wedding. While Grady had asked Claude, Caleb and his cousin, Max to stand. She anticipated a small wedding on a tropical island on the beach with palm trees and an outdoor reception. It helped her to fall back to sleep and she woke in time to catch her flight. Her luggage was light since she had more summer apparel this time.

She heard the engine of Grady's hired car pull up and honk while her door buzzed. She knew that it was him and lugged her bags down the stairs until he met her halfway to assist.

"Morning, dear. Lovely to see you. Thank you," she muttered as she passed him the luggage obligingly. "They are not that heavy."

"Hey, lovely to see you too," he replied as he greeted her and took the baggage. "No, they are fine. Let's get these to the car," he replied.

The chauffer was right on hand to pick up the bags and placed them in the trunk. They hopped in and drove straight to JFK. The morning was beautiful as the plush summer greenery on the way up brought an aroma of a fresh summer morning.

The flight was memorable as they were catered to in business class and had a romantic lunch over the Atlantic.

Grady appeared a bit distracted at one point.

"What is the matter?" Kascey asked.

"Not much. I am still thinking about the Jacob Commerciale deal that has gone sour. I will not bother to stop by the office on our way through Paris. I think that I have said all that I need to on the matter really."

"I know; besides, we will not have time. It is best that you move on from it. There are so many others on the horizon, right?" she responded to console him.

"Yes, there is a new data IPO on the horizon in a few weeks. Once again Claude and I will be working on it. It should be wrapped up by the end of September," he reassured her.

"Which is almost here from my perspective. I have so much to do, and I do not want to think about." In honesty, she was overjoyed by the prospect of the trip to have more ideas from the contemporary feel of the continent. She would see which colors were popular and the trends of the south to incorporate into her designs. As she thought more and more, a design popped in her head, and she immediately sketched it on the napkin.

"Look at you," he exclaimed. "I cannot believe that an idea has just popped into your head and that you are sketching already," he said amazed.

"I know. I just could not help it. We should go on these trips more often."

"We sure should," he replied thinking of the major trip planning that they have for the wedding and the honey moon.

The time flew as it was almost 1 p.m. when they touched down. Kascey adjusted her watch to seven. "Can you believe the time? We shall have a late dinner tonight."

"Yes. I think that we should go to the one we like off the Champs Élysées," suggested Grady.

"Right. Sounds perfect," she responded as the plane taxied to the gate and they pulled their bags from the overhead.

They disembarked and easily found their luggage, and a taxi drove them to the hotel. Kascey was mesmerized by the charming city as they approached the center. She looked around and it was bustling with people in the evening.

They checked into a lovely two-room suite with a lovely view of the Eiffel Tower which was brightly lit.

"Now, this is how you live," Grady commented.

"Oh. It is beautiful—and look at the perfect chaise lounge near the balcony," exclaimed Kascey as she drew open the curtains to take a photo.

"Here allow me," he offered as he extended his arm to grasp the camera to take a photo of her near the balcony.

"Thank you, dear. I really appreciate it."

"My pleasure," he responded as he took the photo of her beaming broadly for the camera.

"I'll send it to Mom and Pop," she teased as they giggled.

The two rushed to have dinner while the restaurants were still open. They sauntered arm in arm along the well-lit street to the side street where they last ate in March.

"It is so quaint and so lovely. Isn't it?" Kascey commented.

"Yes, and I am starving," he replied as he opened the door and she walked in.

The two sat at a lovely table in the corner which was dimly lit by a candle on the checkered table cloth. Customarily, they could hear the violinist as he played. It took her back to the evening that they got engaged and how she would say yes a thousand times over. During the course of the evening, she leaned forward to hear him speak and responded directly as if he were the only person in the world.

His voice often rose above the background music as he spoke about his aspirations.

"I really would like to have two children with you —a boy and a girl. I will leave the names up to you of course —within reason," he said smirking.

"Really, that sounds splendid, but I would like to wait at least a year or two until my business takes off," she responded cautiously.

"Yes, we can do that. There is no real rush. I just assumed that you would like to get a head start," he reasoned.

"Of course. I have thought of names. I think I would want to use Ross if it is a boy and McKenna if it is a girl. At least that would be one of the names. I would like to use one or two of my family names for instance—maybe Ethan after my father."

"Whatever you would prefer. We can go over it more when the time comes," she negotiated. "Right. Now where is the food?" she looked around in anticipation.

"I do not know. It seems to be pretty busy here tonight. I suppose we are lucky that we got a table at such short notice," Grady commented.

"Well, I suppose pretty soon, they are usually quick with the food." She had ordered the duck, and he ordered the lamb. They were starving from the long day's journey. "What time do we leave for Monaco?"

"Possibly at about twelve o' clock because we have a long trip down. So we should get to the airport at about ten or eleven o clock."

"Sounds good. I cannot wait." Monte Carlo was new to her, and she had heard of the quaint, picturesque and historical town. She had been to Cannes and was looking forward to the new beaches to explore in the south. The city lights began to dim as it grew late. By the time they received their check, it was almost eleven. They had sat and chatted half the night and continued after dinner. The view from the hotel was spectacular; they could see the entire city from their eighteenth-century styled-style living room.

Sunday mornings would be rather lethargic since many stores were still closed. She thought of a lovely trip to the museums, and Grady had suggested a ride along the Seine or perhaps a tour to explore the French country side. Whatever the outcome, her working world and worries seemed far behind and yet still so close. The guilt still singed from leaving Vasquez and the anticipation surged of starting fresh in a few weeks. In only a few weeks, she would be live and online, and hopefully back in a few years for shows of her own.

"The last time we were here, I was so worried about the nicked dresses and look how it all unfolded. Can you believe that was only five months ago?"

"No. I really cannot believe that it was. It was only five months ago that we had that horrible

IPO from Jacob Commerciale. By the way, I will not have time to go into the office here. This is just purely vacation—with a little shop talk, right?"

"Right, but I must admit. I really want to have a look at the shops before we go. So, if we could browse the shops on our way to the museums, that would be splendid," she suggested.

"Sure thing. Now who wants to order breakfast?" he asked.

"Sounds good, although I am not that hungry," she admitted.

After croissants, brioche, and coffee in the ornate breakfast room, they decided to wander the streets. They took photographs as they walked from the street near the hotel to the museums. There were so many exhibits to choose from, but they settled on the Jordaens to start. Kascey knew the museum very well, but each time she went, there was something new to discover. They walked through the exhibit, appreciating the realism and contours of his work. Some large paintings were on display, and Grady sized up the financial value of each one.

He teased, "Wouldn't you like to have one of these as a wedding present?"

"I sure would, but which would you choose?"

"I think the largest and the most expensive," he said.

"Really?" she responded, "Why am I not surprised?"

"Because you know me," he said as he jokingly wrapped his arm around her and they moved along the exhibition. Kascey ordered the earphones to listen to the commentators of the exhibition.

"I am getting bit hungry. I think it is almost breakfast time for us."

"Okay," he said a bit relieved. "Why don't we stop by the little café for a coffee—and then we can do more sightseeing. I really have not had a chance to go around town on the bus," he suggested.

"All right. I really want to see another exhibition later. It is just next door." She coaxed. Having the art around her inspired her creativity in her designs and the more that she saw, the more creative she felt.

They wandered in the café, sipped coffee and reminisced about the journey thus far. She felt nostalgic about their last day in Paris before venturing to the next town.

"I still think that this ring is so gorgeous," she said admiring the way it glistened in the sun's afternoon rays.

"I think that it suits you so well," he said as he held her hand to admire it.

"I really hope I do not lose it."

"Oh, just put it in the safe when we get to the hotel in Monaco. We have a boat trip planned around the coast and some sightseeing. I thought that I would surprise you," he announced.

"Truly? I am so excited. I cannot wait. I have been meaning to ask something. Do you think that Lucinda will bring her new boyfriend to the wedding? I mean seeing that she will be standing with Caleb?"

"I think so. I do not see a problem with it. Do you?"

"No. I do not actually. It is just that I do not want any awkwardness with Caleb?" She commented.

"I see. Well, no. I think that he is resolved to the fact now that he knows about Nate. I think that Nate is a great guy."

"Do you really? I really do not know him," she responded uncertain.

"Yes. I think so. Anyway, we shall get to know him better at the wedding in any event," he assured her.

The afternoon flew as they returned from the museum tour. It was already close to four and the streets were crowded again. She took in the last of the afternoon air as they browsed the shops. She tried on a cream leather jacket and impulsively purchased it. "This will go well with my outfit tonight," she joked as the cashier handed it to her.

"I cannot believe you sometimes," he remarked.

"I know," she conceded and laughed.

The evening went smoothly as they chose dinner at a restaurant closer to the hotel in a back street. It was cozy with traditional tablecloths and candles on the tables. They sat as the evening unraveled in front of them.

"This menu looks so delicious; come on we must try the mussels. Everyone seems to have some," suggested Grady.

"Umm," she responded inquisitively as she pondered the menu, "Sure, but then I will order the sole. It looks so good."

"Now that looks good, but I will have the duck," he responded not being able to pass over such an enticing course when in town.

"Okay. We have to promise each other that we have wedding planning. I feel as though I am being immersed in this environment, and I am completely forgetting what I have to do. I am so looking forward to the flight to get myself together," she stated.

"Just relax. There will be plenty of time to get it together. The purpose of the trip is to have a break before everything starts," he said cautiously and also beginning to feel the strain.

"All right. Okay. I know that it will start soon. I will try to relax for now," she conceded.

"Yes. Now where is the waiter? It is time to order." He turned until he saw the waiter arrive.

They placed their orders and enjoyed themselves until the courses were ready. The meal was so enticing as they finished their plates.

Kascey thought of the sunny southern region and was excited as they were close to embarking on the second part of their journey.

Chapter 18

FUN IN THE SUN

The sunny continental August cast an enticing spell as Grady and Kascey looked out the window of the commuter jet which would take them to the small airport of the southern district. It flew past the city and they then passed over the beautiful pastures of the continent. The afternoon sun shone through their window.

"Look how beautiful and quaint. We should really take a country tour next time!" exclaimed Kascey.

"Yes, we really should I can't wait to get to Monaco. It is so beautiful. You will see," replied Grady.

"I bet. I have read so much about it, and I have done so much research for the trip," she responded eagerly.

"It is fantastic, you will see," he promised.

He had not been in a few years, but remembered the classic medieval and renaissance architecture of the large city, its beautiful blue coast and quaint boats anchored to the ancient docks. He knew that she would love it and it was a city which blossomed with romance.

"How long before we land?" she asked.

"Not long now—probably half an hour," he replied as he drew close to her and they leaned toward the window. It seemed as if they had left New York weeks ago, whereas it had only been three days. They were worlds away from their hectic daily lives.

The plane landed and they disembarked. It was already mid-afternoon and airy. The town seemed vast as they drove from the airport to their hotel on the coast. Kascey saw a type of blue water that she had never seen before and snapped photos as she was sure that she would not see it for a while. She felt inspired by the natural colors of the sea for her designs. The hotel had a pre-war appearance with Renaissance accents. She was amazed by its grandiose appearance and charm.

"Lovely choice. It is beautiful," she noticed as they left the taxi.

The porters dutifully carried the luggage as they entered the magnificent lobby.

Kascey knew the beach was not far away. The two were in awe of their quarters as they freshened up before sightseeing. The city was as beautiful and idyllic as a postcard. She had always wanted to go because it always looked so historic and regal. They walked through the center where there were stately buildings and toward the marina where they stopped and had a beautiful view.

"I think that we are so lucky to be doing this. Just look at us. Here we are at the end of the summer on the brink of all that we have going, and we are visiting this beautiful city," perceived Kascey.

"I know, and we really do have a lot on our plates. I mean with the new business and with the wedding to plan and our housing plans. I really want us to get a new place together in midtown and closer to amenities such as schools so that we can start a family," stated Grady fully aware of his five-year plan.

"Yes. That sounds so promising. I mean. I really like your place, but maybe we should have a place of our own to start a family sooner rather than later, and also it will be closer to my studio right?"

"Right, but it will be farther away from my office downtown. I do not really mind that because I can commute and eventually we will have to move to the suburbs like Connecticut and then I will really be commuting," he suggested.

"I know, but I will be commuting also, I suppose by then I will be able to work from home, but this is a bit further in the future."

"Yes, and by then, hopefully you will have many branches and other bases for the business. Let's not get ahead of ourselves." He drew closer to her and asked, "I am wondering where you would like to spend our honeymoon?"

"Well, I do not really know. I suppose in this part of the world. Since we are getting married on an island, I guess we should stick with here—or maybe Italy," she suggested.

"Brilliant suggestion," he replied smiling. "I love you so much—beyond words—and I am thrilled that we will be spending our lives together."

"I love you too, and I do not know what I would have done had it not been me. We are meant to be."

"It was always you. You need not worry about that," he reassured her.

"What is on the menu? It all looks so good and fresh since we are so near the sea.

"Yes. It does look fantastic. Let's get a few things to share. I really want to try everything since we do not have that much time here," he suggested already famished.

"Okay. That sounds like a good plan." The key to the relationship was that they always were in agreement and were compatible. She was able to be with him with such ease. They always had an easy time together and hardly bickered. It was a perfect relationship where one could always pacify the other.

They ordered the calamari and lobster salad and gazed upon the declining sun from the restaurant's deck. It seemed as if they had stayed for hours and the afternoon and evening just slipped away.

Grady looked at her as she appeared inquisitive, and said, "Tell me what you are thinking?"

"Just how much everything has changed since we were on holiday last. I mean we were worried about the dress theft, and you were so supportive. Now here we are again. You are being so supportive again as my fiancé. Thank you."

"No worries. It is what I am here for—besides, you have made me the happiest man in the world. I cannot wait until we are married in December." He was always certain of what he wanted and their relationship was it.

"I do not mean to change the subject, but since I am on the last trip, I have spoken to Vasquez and they have found the people responsible for the theft. Luckily, it will be an easy process and they have been charged. It was a rival Internet seller who wanted to make an easy dollar, I suppose. It is amazing how cruel some people can be," she explained.

"Well that is good news—and now you can put that behind you. You see? I told you it was not your fault after all. Wasn't I right?"

Kascey nodded. She knew that he had such reasoning and she supposed it was because he had lived in the environment for longer than she had. "I know that Vasquez is relieved, and it could not have happened at a worse time to go through it all just as I am leaving."

"I know, but people move on. You cannot stay in the same place forever when you have the talent to do it as well. Maybe that would work for someone else, but your situation is different." He was adamant in his advice. He knew that she had so much talent if only she would believe in herself.

They continued to eat and sip their drinks as the night fell. Their relationship had blossomed into something more endearing during the trip, and she felt as if she had made the right decision to marry him. The two wandered back along the quaint streets and decided to take a taxi the rest of the way. The city was alive at night as the taxi drove past ancient buildings and back to the hotel.

The bellman quickly attended to them as the disembarked.

As they walked through the lobby, he said, "It is going to be a beautiful night, why don't we sit in the lobby and have some aperitifs?"

"Sounds marvelous," Kascey replied with a smile.

The couple sat and listened to the authentic music overlooking the water. The sea shimmered as the city lights reflected on the ripples of the water. Grady glanced at the beautiful view of the water as they continued their conversation.

* * *

Vasquez relished the last few days of summer with family and friends in the Hamptons. His life was full of changes. His sons played and ran along the beach as he pondered the coming months.

"What is wrong, dear?" Daphne asked as she approached the barbecue with the surf and turf.

"Oh. It is so sad that the summer has come to an end and as usual, my agenda is booked," he replied.

"You will see that you can handle it—you always do," she responded.

He looked at her appreciatively. They had the same conversation every year, and she always convinced him that it would work out. However, this year was different. It was to be without his right hand assistance, Kascey, and so he had reason for concern.

"I know, but this is a different year. Kascey leaves the week after next—just before the fall show and the holiday season sales. This is a different year, he expressed.

"I know. Surely you can make it without her. Look at your talent. You have new staff with a different type of experience in where the company is heading. You must have more confidence that this will work. You will see. When you go in next week, you probably will not notice the difference," Daphne reasoned.

"Also, there is the issue with the dress theft and that whole ordeal. Now that they have found the people responsible and such low lives at that. How will I ever get over it? It is so hard not having people you can trust."

"Do not worry. It will all sort itself out, dear. You will see. Now try to take your mind off it and concentrate on the here and now and our lovely weekend," Daphne said.

"Thank you once again. What would I do without you?" He said as he walked over to give her a lasting hug.

They placed the seafood and vegetables on the grill and called the children over for lunch.

* * *

The Chisholm family gathered at *Silent Manor* for the weekend. Lucinda, Trudy, Nate, and Aunt

Mavey were there too. It was as if they were back in time.

Kelly and Jane worked in the open kitchen as they were to have a large lunch at the formal dining table.

Damien sat with his feet up on the lounge and read the town's newspapers recently delivered. Mavey is Kelly's sister who has worked in marketing for years and lives in upstate New York.

"Are the others back yet from town?" asked Kelly as she peered from the preparations to her husband.

"No, not yet," he responded and got back to reading.

Nate, Lucinda, and Trudy had driven to town to shop for a few more items for the dessert. It was their last day in the Cape until the holidays, and they wanted to make it memorable. Lucinda drove the convertible to the quaint sea town where she had spent many of her childhood years.

"Oh, they should be here soon, I guess," she responded.

"Yes. It should not be long now," added Mavey who had spent many years with the family since being widowed.

"I wonder how Grady and Kascey are doing?" Kelly called out to her husband. "Have you heard from them, Damien?"

"No, not a word since he phoned from the office last Friday."

"I hope they are all right," she said worried.

"I'm sure they are fine," expressed Mavey said. "They are on holiday together." She looked at her sister as if to say stop meddling, and preferred the laissez faire approach.

"Yes, I am sure that you are right. I will wait to hear from them."

* * *

Lucinda sat behind the wheel of the convertible. Nate was beside her, and Trudy was in the back with her luxurious red hair being lambasted by the wind. Nate was enamored by his surroundings and was on the upside of a lovely weekend with Lucinda's family. They drove along the winding road of the sleepy seaside village now closer to *Silent Manor.* The scent of the ocean encircled and the sun started its warm glow which began to glisten on the car's surface. Lucinda pulled into the drive way as the parties disembarked the vehicle.

"Hello, hello we are back," Lucinda announced as they entered the front door with the packages.

"Hello, dear. We were just wondering where you all were," responded Kelly concerned.

"Really? We just took a drive along the shore. I wanted to show Nate the scenery. Sorry."

"Yes. It was fantastic. There is such lovely scenery around here. It must have been perfect spending vacations here," Nate added.

"It surely has been. We have had so many great times here, and I have so many fond memories," responded Kelly.

Nate was such a charming young man that it was difficult to place the blame on him for anything. Trudy remained silent as Lucinda received a bit of her chiding while Damien sat submerged in his reading and not very concerned. Jane pulled the contents out of the bag and added them to the rest of the items to prepare.

"We were just wondering if you have heard from your brother, Luce?" Aunt Mavey asked nonchalantly.

"No, but I am sure we can check for status updates. I am sure that they are having a brilliant time. I mean who wouldn't?" she replied looking at Nate and laughing.

"You are right. We should leave the lovebirds alone—but you know how close we are," Mavey replied.

"Yes, I do, replied Lucinda who then turned to Jane and asked, "Would you like some help with the veggies? You know how good I am."

"No, thanks. We are all set here. Just worry about your guests. We have it all sorted on this end, dear," Jane replied with a wink knowing that she was merely trying to impress Nate.

"So, Nate, why don't you come and have a seat? The Open is on," Damien said.

"Thanks. It sounds good. How is the weather in New York?" replied Nate taking him up on his invitation.

"It seems bright and sunny as usual for August," replied Damien.

"Fabulous. We had some beautiful weather in Connecticut this past week," he continued.

"Nate, would you like something to drink?" Lucinda asked.

"No thanks, Luce. I am fine for now." He tried to avoid her having to do too much after the scenic tour. Trudy went to finish packing as it would be only a little while after brunch that they would head out on the boat.

When the meal was prepared, everyone assembled at the table and sipped the mimosa while tucking into the quiche.

"This is delicious as usual," commented Mavey savoring each bite.

"Yes. Thanks, Jane. It is all so fabulous," added Luce, quick not to forget her manners.

"Yes. It tastes wonderful," commented Nate quickly remembering his manners and willing to make an impression.

"Come and have a seat, Jane. I think that we have gotten everything now," invited Kelly. Kelly and Jane had grown closer over the years, and there was so much excitement about the upcoming nuptials in the family.

"So, any more news about the wedding?" asked Mavey.

"No, has anyone heard anything?" asked Kelly very interested. The others motioned their heads in the negative and looked at one another.

"No, and I am standing. So, when I hear more, I will let you know," replied Lucinda.

"Sounds like a good plan," answered Mavey. She was very excited because she had no children of her own and counted Grady as her own son. "I bet we are all looking forward to somewhere warm and sunny for a few days."

"That is right. They sure know how to pick a location," added Kelly, "Well, Luce, if you ever get married you should do it in the spring."

"Sure, Mom. Sounds great," responded Lucinda. The family discussed the wedding more and lounged around the veranda for the rest of the day.

Everyone returned to work after the weekend break and long summer and there was much planning to get underway. Kascey did not renew her lease and had a farewell gathering at the studio. She said her sincerest good-byes to Vasquez who gave her some advice. Within weeks, her business was established; orders came in from all over the country. Grady had provided the funding through investors for her and made the initial startup far less stressful than what could have been. He threw a small soiree to celebrate her opening which included a few colleagues, staff, and investors. Kascey was overwhelmed her first week and missed her former colleagues, but ploughed through the first week conscientiously.

Meanwhile, Kascey had the wedding planner working diligently for the wedding in December. The invitations were almost ready to be sent, and the flights and hotels were being reserved for the guests. The dresses were still being designed, and a fitting was planned a few weeks before the wedding. There was still so much to do until then, and her work was taking precedent.

Chapter 19
THE FEAST

The season swept upon the city in its usual fashion with its festive lights providing warmth in the cold evening air. It had become frigidly cold the days running up to Thanksgiving. A new mood had overcome the city as it did each year at that time. The evenings grew mystical and darker, and Kascey worked diligently to complete the next season's collection.

Sire and Judy worked persistently beside her, aware of the pending deadlines. The couture line still had strong Internet sales success, and orders were coming in by the dozens. It had been a few months since she had started, and with the planning of the wedding, it was as if she did not have time to think. It was already evening, and she was meeting Grady at their regular restaurant in the Flatiron District.

"I am afraid we have to start wrapping up," she stated with determination to get moving. "I am meeting Grady for dinner." It was such exhilaration to finally admit to her own plans on her own time. It was well deserved, and after all, he did take an interest in her enterprise. She thought about how much they had achieved during the long fall days and how driven he was to get her business moving.

"Oh, fabulous. That sounds wonderful. Have a nice time," Sire responded as he examined the screen in front of him and Judy started to fold the fabric.

"Okay, have a nice time," added Judy as she confirmed, "We will lock up."

Kascey's trust had grown immeasurably since they started, and she appreciated her assistants' motivation even though they had only been with her for a few months. She left them figuratively glued to their chairs, and knew that more staff was needed.

The evening air blew a chill across her face as she took a taxi to the small Italian restaurant in the Village. When she arrived, she could see Grady's silhouette seated in the corner and waiting patiently.

He stood as she walked in closer to him. "Hello, dear. How are you? I hope that you have not been waiting long?" she greeted him warmly.

"No. I just got here. We also had a long day at the office. How was your day?" He asked intently.

"It was fine. I am so pleased with it all. Thank you," she responded warmly. "How was your day then?" She was eager to hear.

"Busy, as usual. Claude and I are working on another new IPO for an electronics gaming company. It is all going well," he said.

She could not believe that he always had such interesting projects and such a vast array of knowledge in every industry. He never ceased to amaze her. On the other hand, he looked at her and could not believe that in one month they would be newlyweds. He was still amazed by her.

"So, are you ready to go to Maine for Thanksgiving? We leave on Wednesday night, remember?"

It was only a day away, and she still had so much to complete. "Yes, of course. I am looking forward to it," she responded contently knowing what she had planned for the weekend filled with shopping. "I am sure you are aware that this is my busiest time of the year?" She explained.

"Yes. It shall only be for the day. We get back on Friday and just relax, everyone takes time for Thanksgiving," he added knowing all that he had on his plate at work as well.

"I know. It is just that there is so much to do with this being my first holiday with the company and, it will be hard to tear myself away," she admitted.

"I know, but Kelly is expecting you. And you know how much you love the house there. I am sure you that you will want to go over the wedding with everyone. This is a bizarre year for us, but we can do this." He reached over and held her hand as an art of persuasion.

"Of course, of course. I am so excited. I am sure that it will all be marvelous," she conceded as she smiled at him.

"Great. What will we have this time? I think that we are running out of options." She examined the menu.

"I will have the usual Clam Vongole. It is awesome here," he added.

The couple ordered and ate quickly because it had gotten late and Grady was on his way back to work at that hour.

"By the way, I have read your statements and Kascey Kann Couture is doing really well so far. I thought that I would let you know to inspire you. Keep up the good work."

She smiled at him appreciatively, "I really needed that. Thank you. We have been working hard, and I need to hire someone else for the holidays. Do you think that I should see if," she paused, for a minute she was thinking of Mari or Moda and knew that it would not be a prospect. She respected Vasquez too much and she really missed him during the holidays. She had spent her first Thanksgiving with the company years ago in Westchester and was looking forward to traveling to Maine for this one.

*   *   *

Kascey felt the customary wintry New England air as she and Grady entered the taxi at the airport. It was already nine in the evening on Thanksgiving eve, and she and Grady had a hectic time at the airport filled with holiday travelers escaping an approaching storm. They drove to the childhood home where the man of her dreams spent his Thanksgivings, and this year would be no exception for him. The classic New England colonial-styled wooden homes lined Maine Street and one was reminded of the quaint boating passtime in the village. They pulled up to a yellow house with fairy lights around the doorframe and a holiday swag on the front.

"Oh, it is so beautiful as usual," she commented.

Damien heard the rustle in the driveway and went out to help them. He had fond memories of his son's visits through the years like this one. After dinner, they would play touch football and the excitement crept in as there were only a few more weeks until Christmas.

"Hello, hello. Glad that you finally got here," Damien said as he embraced his son and Kascey. "Here, let me help with that," he said as he picked up a few bags while Grady paid the taxi driver.

"Everything is beautiful as usual. Thank you for inviting me again," Kascey commented as they walked inside.

"Thank you for coming. It is our pleasure— believe me—and Kelly is so excited. She is still in the kitchen, and she has been there all day.

Lucinda comes in the morning with Nate, and Kelly's sister is here, and of course, Jane is too." It brought back memories for Damien of when the house was filled with family and college friends of his children. Now it was a different type of holiday, and they still had more celebrations in the form of a wedding in the tropics before the Christmas season.

Grady and Kascey walked through the traditionally decorated home to the back kitchen where three ladies worked diligently.

"Hello, dears!" exclaimed Kelly as she looked up from rolling some dough.

Grady walked over and kissed his mother, his aunt, and Jane, "Hello, yes, we have arrived. We had to fly before the storm. I hope that it won't be too bad for Lucinda in the morning," he said concerned.

"Oh, I hope not too," Kelly kissed back, slightly worried. "How was the trip?"

"Fine, fine," he said as he greeted them all.

Kascey approached to greet Kelly and Mavey who were peeling potatoes while Jane was wiping the counters.

"Hello, dear. It's great to see you." She greeted them most enthusiastically. "Now, you and Grady have a seat in the family room while we get this sorted. There is no pressure; we have it all sorted. I am sure you have had a hectic day at work." Kelly was so understanding, and also liked control so they followed her suggestions.

"Of course. Just let me know if there is anything that I can do to help," Kascey responded. It was the same every year. She was treated so well and loved coming.

The aroma of spices and pumpkin filled the home as they settled in their rooms. They then met Damien in front of the TV reading the newspaper. Kascey was knackered and could not wait to rest while Grady checked his Blackberry on the settee.

"So, any more plans for the wedding?" asked Damien.

"Yes, Kascey anymore plans?" asked Grady as he referred the question to her.

"Well, we have numbers. Seventy people will be attending. It's not a small wedding by any means. I think they all want to be in Bimini in December. That is my guess."

"I see. That is a lot. Where are they all coming from?" asked Damien

"Mainly, they are our friends since we have such a small family. So, they are coming from the Northeast and some from Canada," responded Kascey. "Workmates and staff are coming, therefore; the numbers have risen. Even Vasquez is coming, and I am so very excited."

"That many? Well, we will have a fantastic time," Damien answered cheerfully.

"Yes, we sure will," added Grady excited.

"How are your parents, Kascey?" Damien asked.

"They are great. I just spoke to them, and they send their love to you all."

"Well, we send our love back," ensured Damien.

"Yes, we will all catch up in December, which is a short while away. We are all booked now. We just need you to show up, dear," he joked.

"I wouldn't miss it for the world," she commented in a mocking manner.

The group watched television while Mavey, Jane, and Kelly popped in and out of the family and dining rooms to prepare for the feast.

Grady fell asleep on the couch, and Kascey retired to the guest room and fell asleep there.

* * *

It was a crisp morning where bright beams of light from the snow and sun lit the pale green walls of the bedroom. It had a traditional New England style with homemade quilts and cushions, wood-paneled floors, and crocheted rugs. Kascey walked over to the whitewashed armoire and prepared for the day. She had slept late as it was almost ten, and she could hear talking and laughing from below. When she was completely dressed, she decided to go downstairs.

Kelly and Jane had laid out a continental styled buffet for breakfast. They set out homemade cinnamon buns, bran and cranberry muffins, fresh orange juice, and freshly brewed coffee.

"Happy Thanksgiving! Oh, this is marvelous. What a lovely spread!" she stated to Kelly as she wished her a splendid morning.

"Happy Thanksgiving to you too. Please help yourself. We thought that we would have a small breakfast because there is so much food coming in a few hours," she responded.

"Morning, dear. How did you sleep?" Grady asked as he winked at her.

"Rather well. Happy Thanksgiving," she replied coyly.

"Happy Thanksgiving," he whispered as he kissed her cheek.

"Glad to hear it," Kelly said. "Has anyone heard from Lucinda and Nate? They should have taken their flight by now?"

"Not yet. I suppose she will send word soon, dear," responded Damien. "Happy Thanksgiving, everyone," he stated as he poured more coffee. His phone beeped as he went to sit down. "Oh, here we are, dear, she has just sent word that they have landed,"

"Fabulous. Okay, we are all on schedule for a one thirty start," directed Kelly as Jane nodded from the kitchen.

The crowd relaxed over breakfast and then dispersed to get ready for the afternoon feast.

Kascey decided to wear her cream cashmere top with a pearl-embedded collar and her burgundy wool skirt. The atmosphere was frosty, and snow lined the roofs of homes down the block. As she exited the room to descend the stairs, she could hear Lucinda's voice. It was a cheerful voice to which she had become accustomed.

"Well look at you. Happy Thanksgiving!" Lucinda remarked as she drew closer to see her.

"Happy Thanksgiving to you too! I am so glad that you arrived safely. Hello, Nate. Happy Thanksgiving!" Exclaimed Kascey said.

"Happy Thanksgiving!" He responded. "So, I hear that you and Grady got here last night."

"Yes, that is right. We tried to beat the rush, but it was still very crowded. Hopefully, it will not be in the morning. So, how was your flight?" she asked.

"It went rather well, and it was not as crowded as we thought it would be," Lucinda replied. "Actually, we have some news," she confessed.

Kascey's mouth dropped open. "Are you serious?" She looked at her in amazement and then looked over at Nate rather pleased.

"Yes, look." Lucinda held up the oval platinum diamond ring on her finger.

"Well, it is lovely. When did this happen?" Kascey asked.

"It happened last night. We had a lovely dinner, and then it happened. She was beside herself and overjoyed as she kept peering at Nate.

"Actually, I wanted to wait until today, but I got anxious," Nate admitted proudly. "She still said yes," he continued.

"I sure did," she responded completely enamored.

"I am so happy for you both. Aren't we, Grady?"

"Yes, congratulations again. It is fabulous news. Nate, we are pleased to have you in the family." Kascey looked over at him as to say, *did you know?* He shook his head in shock and she did not feel so sidelined.

"Oh, there you are, dear," Kelly said as she placed some hors d'oeuvres on the buffet table.

"Yes, do you need any help?" asked Kascey.

"Oh no, please relax. Damien will get you a drink, and we will be serving soon. Everyone, here are some hors d'oeuvres to get us started. Dinner will be in one hour. Save some room," she advised.

"Thank you, Kelly," replied Kascey.

"Thanks, Mom," her children replied.

"Thanks, Mrs. Chisholm," replied Nate. He was still very new to the situation as it was his first Thanksgiving with them.

"Kascey, did she tell you?" Kelly asked.

"Yes. I heard," she replied still shocked.

"Well, we found out last night, but we wanted it to be a surprise. It looks as if we are planning two weddings now," responded Kelly.

"I know. It's fabulous."

"Yes. I only just found out," teased Grady as he looked over at Kascey.

"I wanted to surprise everyone, and I figured this would be the best time to do it," admitted Lucinda.

"It is so pleasant," responded Kascey.

"Right. I shall get back to the kitchen with Mavey and Jane. We shall be seated shortly," stated Kelly overjoyed.

"Could you grab me a few hors d'oeuvres, dear?" Grady was a bit shocked that his sister was now engaged to a man he did not know very well and with whom he had not spent much time.

"Can I get anyone any beverages? Asked Damien from the kitchen.

"No, thank you. I will wait for dinner," responded Kascey.

"Sure, Dad. I will have a beer," responded Grady rather quickly.

"Anything from the bar? Luce? Nate?" asked Damien.

"Thanks, Dad. I'll have a glass of Chardonnay please," responded Lucinda.

"No, thank you," replied Nate still on his best behavior.

"Sure thing. Coming right up!" Damien promised.

Grady could see through Nate's timidity. He had been there and knew that he would be feeling extremely comfortable soon. He watched the football game on TV, and Kascey sat beside him.

"Are you all right, dear?" she asked.

"Yes, fine. The game is just getting started. How are you?"

"Great, just great," she smiled as she slightly patted his arm.

Lucinda and Nate sat on the sofa. She said, "Now we can plan together. Have you got it all ready yet? Are we having a fitting next week?"

"Yes. It is all coming together, thanks. We are having a fitting next Thursday. They are bringing the dresses to the studio. Also, we are having 70 people. I have the planner booking the resort places, so send your preferences to her so that she can accommodate you. The honeymoon is booked for boxing day, the day after Christmas, and we are done."

"That's great," Lucinda said. "Have you decided on a place to live? I remember you had been viewing apartments?"

"Not yet. I think that Kascey will move in downtown after the wedding. Isn't that right, Kascey?"

"Yes, that is right. We are going to take our time—depending on how much space we will need?" agreed Kascey.

"Sounds good," responded Lucinda said.

"So, have you a date in mind yet?" asked Kascey.

"Well, it is still a bit early. We were thinking early April—perhaps on the Cape," she replied nodding while Nate nodded in agreement rather excitedly.

"Okay, here we are, folks. One for you, Luce and one for you, Grady," said Damien as he handed them their drinks. "Your mother says that we can start to get seated in the dining room. The turkey is almost done."

"Thanks, Dad," Grady said as he picked up his glass.

Mavey, Kelly, and Jane started to bring out the dishes of the feast. There was everything imaginable. Green beans, stuffing, mashed sweet potatoes, cranberry sauce, beets, peas, and at last the turkey which Kelly carried proudly. It was the feast that all had been waiting for as they gathered around the table and took their seats.

Now it is a tradition that we say what we are thankful for this holiday. So please let us start," Kelly said.

Damien started, "I am thankful that we have a lovely meal each year with our children who have decided to expand this family."

Mavey continued, "I am thankful for lovely nieces and nephews and family to share this day."

Jane said, "I am thankful to come here each year and to have this family like my own."

Kelly nodded in appreciation.

"I am thankful that all of my dreams have come true this year," Grady stated as he looked at Kascey.

"I am grateful to all of you, and to Grady for being my fiancé and for promising me a beautiful life," asserted Kascey.

"I am thankful to have a new family and that Lucinda has agreed to be my wife," Nate said.

"I am thankful for all of you for accepting Nate as one of the family," Lucinda added teary eyed. "Thank you, Nate."

Kelly and Jane wiped away their tears as it was a rather emotional celebration of achieving hopes and overcoming fears while having new people in their lives.

"Now, let us all dig in," directed Kelly. She looked over at Damien amazed that so much had been accomplished in one year for the family. Outside grew darker as three o' clock approached. It was time for the apple, pecan, and pumpkin pie with ice cream for dessert. It was the homemade vanilla from the local store with natural maple syrup. The crowd sat, ate and chatted until late in the evening. They exchanged family stories of old and some new. It was a day of remembering Thanksgivings past and now present, while envisioning the possibility of the Thanksgivings in the future and the wonders they would bring.

Kascey and Grady left the following morning to face the most important shopping day of the year. For her, the season was about promotions and sales, but she was lucky to have his wonderful family to share the beauty of the season. On the way back she smiled and said, "That had to have been the best Thanksgiving I have had. Thank you."

"I know. I really enjoyed it too. There will be many more like that," he promised.

"That would be very well if I can look forward to that every year. Your family is so amazing. They have made me feel so welcome from day one."

"Soon they will be your family too," he replied reassuringly.

The city was majestic as the car drove in the city that Friday. The gorgeous snow lay newly fallen on the sidewalks, and homes were lit at building level in the Village. There was that special holiday feeling.

Kascey held her coat collar to stop the cold air from getting to her. She wished him good-bye, and walked inside her building. They had plans for the weekend, but were eager to get back to work.

Chapter 20
'TIS THE SEASON

It was a week until the wedding and also the busiest shopping period of the year. The staff spent overtime in the studio filling the orders, which were now universal. Mabel was in touch with Kascey frequently regarding the manufacturing of the clothing line at the factory. They also caught up on the latest details for the wedding.

"Dear, we filled that order for you—and it is being shipped to Hong Kong. It should get to the distributor before the holidays," Mabel reassured her daughter.

"Splendid. We are so inundated now that the holidays are upon us. I cannot believe how much time has flown. We are having my bridal shower this weekend, and it is twelve days before the wedding," she said exasperated.

"Have fun—and try not to work too hard. So, have you had the fitting for the dress?" she asked.

"Yes, on Saturday and it is superb. I really love the dress. I cannot wait for you to see it. You will love it," she reassured her.

"*We* cannot wait to see it either. Your father is so excited for the wedding. He is almost packed. Can you believe it?"

"What? Already. I cannot believe it. I think that is great that he is just as excited as I am. It's such an inconvenience that we all have to fly though. I hope that everyone catches their flights because it is so difficult to book at this time of the year. I'm keeping my fingers crossed." She remained hopeful.

"Will all of your friends and coworkers fly at the same time as you will be flying?" She grew inquisitive.

"Some. I want to get in a day earlier. Moda and Grady's sister will be coming in with me, however others have decided to take the Friday flight and the wedding is on Saturday before the holidays." Kascey explained.

"Yes, dear, I think that I remember that now. "We will be in that Friday as well. We cannot wait to see you, dear. It has been since the fall, but we communicate all the time."

"We sure do, now, I must get going. Mondays are always difficult, but. I will call soon."

"All right, dear. If there is anything else you need, please let me know and I can have it arranged for you."

"Thanks, Mom. I really appreciate it. Bye."

"Sure, dear and bye."

Kascey got to her busy day. There was so much on her plate that she was heavily relying on her assistants who were giving her reminders several times per day. It was already December 8, and her wedding was on December 21. She was corresponding with the wedding planner regularly who had the venue and the reception all arranged. The weather was mild in Bimini for that time of the year, and she would have the ceremony on the beach. She could envision it with Grady by her side. That reminded her to check in with him. The interior decorator was at his apartment designing the interior for the master bedroom, which had to be before they left for their honeymoon. She thought of how lucky she was to have support in Judy and Sire during the season. They had agreed to hold down the fort until the wedding was over. She felt guilty leaving them there, but it had to be done.

She called Grady and said, "Hello, dear. How are you?"

"Fine, just fine. I had lunch with Claude and Caleb, and we had our tuxedos fitted. Also, I think that we should at least have Nate as an usher now that he will be my brother-in-law. Can you believe that Luce is planning a spring wedding in the Cape?"

"It sounds fabulous," she responded in anticipation.

"I know, she is tying the knot as we are," he laughed.

"So, how was the fitting?"

"It fit perfectly. Claude and Caleb have tried on theirs and their tuxedos fit too. We are good to go. All that is left is to get there, and hopefully on time—weather permitting."

"What do you mean?" She asked perplexed.

"Nothing, dear. It's just a saying for this time of year. I will charter a plane if I have to."

"Fantastic. Do you have time for dinner tonight?"

"Now, I am in a bind. I do not think so. Sorry. Tomorrow night is fine though."

"Okay. You will get a pass this one time since we are both so busy," she reasoned.

"Thanks. Please do not be so hard on me," he remarked.

"I know. In twelve days, we shall be in married bliss," she responded nostalgically.

"I know. My parents are packed. Can you believe it?"

"Mine are as well. Isn't that funny?" She responded absurdly.

"Yes. It sure is. We must be underrating this whole thing," he joked.

"Probably. Bye now. Take care and I will talk to you later," she signed off.

"Okay. Bye, dear."

Grady was busy with another IPO, which he and Claude wanted to wrap up in a few days in time for the wedding. In all honesty, his apartment looked ransacked and he could not think of the wedding fully. He was lucky that Kascey had made most of the plans—and that they were coming along so smoothly.

* * *

The Saturday before the wedding arrived far more quickly than expected. Moda had planned a bridal shower at a lovely venue in the Flatiron District. The guests included Mari, Moda, Nathalie, Lucinda, Trudy, Corrine, Judy, Sire as well as other staff and friends of Kascey. The venue was decorated in rose pink, cream, and silver ornaments and ribbons for the festive season. There was a distinct NY Saturday afternoon feeling with the bright sunshine to last only a few hours more.

She did not want a surprise and Kascey planned to arrive on time to avoid disappointing the guests.

"Now, I have practically everything packed for next week." She stated as she and Nathalie arrived.

"So have I. I just have to thank you so much for having the wedding in Bimini so that we can have a winter's break while we are at it," she responded chuffed.

"I know, and I get to be married. However, we have to remember to pick up the license as soon as we fly in, a must, really," Kascey replied convincingly.

"Yes, right. Oh, look who is here already!" remarked Nathalie as they walked in to see Moda and Mari already perched on the lounge sofa.

"Hello! How are you?" Kascey exclaimed as she walked closer to embrace them.

"Fine, just fine," responded Moda as she stood towering slightly over the rest.

"Yes," Mari said. "We are great, and it's so lovely to see you. We come bearing gifts," added Mari as she greeted and hugged Kascey and then greeted Nathalie.

"So, are we all ready?" asked Kascey as she took a seat on the settee next to her friends.

"We sure are," replied Moda. "Remy is beside himself and thank you for having him as the photographer. He is so into getting some perfect images for the wedding and on the island," she stated appreciatively.

"It is really my pleasure," Kascey said. "I am so happy that you can make it to my quaint island wedding. Truly." She was so sincere.

"We would not have missed it for the world," Moda replied getting choked up, as the others nodded in agreement.

"Yes. It is such an honor," responded Mari. "We cannot wait," she continued with tears in her eyes as it had been one of the first times to have seen Kascey since she left the company.

The waiter took the drink orders as they waited for the others to arrive.

Trudy and Lucinda pranced in together to see the others now laughing and having their refreshments.

"Look at who is here!" Kascey stated as she looked up from her conversation to see her soon to be sister in law and her best friend. "Hi, Luce!"

"Hello. How are you? And congratulations again!" Lucinda said as she greeted Kascey and met the others.

"Hello to you too, and hello Trudy. How have you been?" asked Kascey as she stood to greet them.

"Perfect—just fabulous and we have one more week to go. Unbelievable!" responded Lucinda.

"I know. I am all packed and have bought a new dress," Trudy replied. "Thank you for the invite. I am so excited."

"It is my pleasure and thank you for coming," Kascey said. "And please have a seat. The waiter should be around again soon to take the orders."

"Oh, thank you," Lucinda replied as they took a seat. "Look here they come with some hors d'oeuvres too."

The ladies sampled the lovely crudités being offered. Kascey had ordered the melon and Parma ham, salmon caviar on bruschetta, vegetarian fritters, and seared beef with wasabi on rye. For dessert, there were coconut balls and sliced vanilla and lemon cream cake.

"Oh my gosh. This all looks so delicious!" exclaimed Lucinda.

Kascey smirked, "I know. Try it all! We can diet later," she suggested to the ladies.

Just then, entered Judy and Sire with gifts, followed by Corrine with some other staff wandering in. Kascey was so excited to see Corrine as she had not seen her in such a long time.

"Hello Corrine," Kascey said. "It is so lovely to see you. It has been ages."

"Yes, it has been and here, I have a bridal present for you. It is such lovely news about you and Grady."

"Well, thank you. It is so kind of you and I am sorry you will not be able to come to the wedding, but we can have lunch when I am back from the honeymoon after the holidays," convinced Kascey.

"You are welcome," Corrine replied. "I am sorry to miss it, but someone has to hold down the fort. You know. It would be lovely to have lunch."

"Oh, fabulous!" she responded. She then looked over at her staff members and greeted them.

Judy and Sire walked over to Kascey and handed her the gifts.

"Hi, here you are," Judy said energetically, "Congratulations! We are looking forward to supporting you in your new life with Grady."

"Thank you. It is so kind of you," she responded.

"Yes, we are very much looking forward to being with you next week, and thank you so much for having us," continued Sire. "It is all going to go well. We have everything under control."

"Thank you for the reassurance, and it is my pleasure to have you. We will have a lovely time. Now have a seat and enjoy the party. There are a few more people to meet."

Everyone gathered around her and sipped their drinks when Lucinda suggested the next agenda on the soiree. "Listen, we have two little games. One is the "newlywed" game, which I am sure you are familiar with, and the other is wedding movie charades. We have some questions to ask our bride about the groom; hopefully she will pass with flying colors," she said as she looked at Kascey hopefully.

"Oh no. Are you going to put me on the spot?" Kascey joked.

"Yes, we are actually. They are so easy. So here goes, the first question is: what is Grady's favorite meal? It is so easy right?"

"Okay. I know this one. It is beef bourguignon? Am I right?"

The crowd grew silent in anticipation.

Lucinda looked at her card. "Yes, that is correct! See? I told you it was easy. Okay, here's the next one. Who was Grady's first kiss?"

The others looked at each other in shock.

Lucinda smiled since she knew that Kascey knew the answer.

"Yes. I know this because he mentioned it before. It was on the Cape the summer of his senior year. Oh, what was her name? Gertrude? I think, right?" she asked uncertain.

"Yes. I can't believe you got that one. Okay, that may have been a bit too easy." Lucinda looked at her cards. "What was the first album he ever bought?"

"I think that I know this one. It is REM, right?"

"Yes, that is correct. Okay, last question." She looked at her cards mischievously as the others burst into laughter.

"What is his favorite movie of all time?"

"It must be *The Usual Suspects,* right?" asked Kascey.

"Yes, you are right and you have done so very well. I cannot believe it."

The group applauded Kascey's success as Lucinda dragged over the large board to the center of the room for the next game.

"All right, everyone. Let's all have some more refreshments before we get to the next game," suggested Kascey as the waiter came over to pour more wine and offer more crudités. She felt as though she deserved it after answering all the questions correctly.

Everyone got into groups and chose someone to approach the board with a movie idea. Moda and Trudy did exceptionally well, adding to the speculation that another wedding would be in their midst.

Moda said, "We hear that you are getting married also, Lucinda. Congratulations!"

"Thank you. Yes. It will be a short engagement, but since the family is in married fever, we thought that we would take the chance," she joked.

"Oh. I am happy it has worked out for you!"

"Yes, and we will send invites after this wedding."

After charades, everyone gathered around the gifts for Kascey to open. She loved all of them; they were so thoughtful. Some were clothing items while others were household that she and Grady could use.

"Thank you all. I love the gifts. I really do. Remember in a week's time, we will be on the island so do not forget to bring your swimsuits."

"Oh, we cannot wait!" exclaimed Mari as she raised her hands in a wide gesture.

"I cannot wait!" Stated Moda.

"Well, thank you all. It has been such a lovely afternoon. I shall always cherish it—and your thoughtfulness."

"Thank you. We will see you in Bimini next week," replied Moda full of emotion.

"Sure thing," added Kascey. Knowing that time she would not be an unmarried woman for much longer.

They spent a bit more time wrapping up the soiree before all the guests trickled out with lovely guest goody bags Moda had prepared.

Kascey extended a hug to her soon-to-be sister-in-law as they all left in appreciation of her efforts. She could not wait to call Grady who was spending the ultimate Saturday working in New York before the holiday season. He had planning of his own and had offered to pitch in for the hotel and travel fees for the wedding. It would have been too much for Kascey to bear alone.

Kascey's week was full of holiday orders and preparations and she did not know how she was going to get through. Luckily, with the assistance of loyal staff which she had. She would be gone for most important dates of the holiday season leading up to December 25, and she had to rely on her loyal staff. Some would remain in New York to hold down the fort while others closer to her would celebrate with Blackberries in hand.

Chapter 21
FLIGHT TIME

Kascey and Grady decided to take the early flight to Bimini from LaGuardia airport. It was an airport that they were familiar with and it was closer to them.

"Are you sure you have everything?" Grady asked as they hopped in the car with the bags.

"Yes. I am pretty sure I do," she replied.

They had four large suitcases between them. Nathalie would be bringing down the dress so that Grady could not see it before the wedding. They were meeting their parents at the resort that evening. Mabel and Ethan had to travel from Toronto, while Kelly and Damien were travelling from Maine to the sunny resort. The couple cleared security and embarked the plane. The pilot stated that the weather was 77 degrees

Fahrenheit and sunny as they looked at each other in excitement.

Grady and Kascey were involved in conversation as they sipped their beverages. Nathalie, Moda, Mari, Claude, Luce, Nate, Caleb, Trudy and Vasquez were expected on the island later that evening. They all decided to take a flight later in the day. Luckily, clear skies were in their favor for flight, and all were expected without delay.

The plane entered crystal blue territory with what looked like aquamarine plots encircling tiny islands as the call was made to prepare for landing. Bimini's terrain and sleepy village could be seen from above. The plane swooped over the island and landed on the runway smoothly. Some of the other passengers clapped and cheered in appreciation and to start their holiday. For Grady and Kascey, it was a short action packed weekend with their closest friends and family. They disembarked while smiling and waving to the crew, and walked to the counters to enter customs. A shuttle bus took them to the resort where they would celebrate their wedded bliss.

Kascey noticed that the temperature was warm yet with a slight breeze. Kascey said, "I hope it will not be too humid for the wedding. I am worried about the dress."

"I am sure it will be fine. The weather tonight for the rehearsal dinner will be clear with a cool breeze. So tomorrow should be fine too. Do not worry," he reassured her. She looked toward the oceanfront as the bus drew closer to the resort, Grady was overwhelmed by how extensive it was and how many people were vacationing at the resort.

"Welcome to Bimini," the valet greeted them as they left the bus and walked to the lobby area which was festively decorated. One could hear the calypso melodies in the background as they were given their separate rooms and handed the keys. They were meant to meet the wedding planner in a few hours in the lobby, and Kascey also wanted to spend some time on the water's edge before her friends and family arrived.

"Thank you," she commented as they were handed the keys and the receptionist replied, "Enjoy your stay."

They were taken to one of the top floors where the bellman showed them their views. Kascey felt sentimental as it was a familiar view and one of the last views that she would see with life as she knew it. Although Grady's presence was more than sufficient, she needed to speak to her Mum. She heard the phone ring.

"Hello, dear. Are you all settled in? I am just checking that you have arrived safely."

"Hello, Mum. That's right. We had a great flight down and we are now at the hotel. I am meeting the wedding planner soon. When do you get in?"

"Our plane leaves Charlotte in a few minutes so, I think that we should reach you by four or so. I had better listen out for the flight call. Love you—and see you soon." Mabel was as excited as any mother of the bride could be and had over-packed for the occasion. She and Ethan left the seating area to embark the plane.

Kascey had already changed into something more tropical that she had designed. Now fully refreshed, she met Grady as they took the elevator to the lobby to meet the wedding planner.

The wedding planner was waiting patiently in the lobby. Kascey recognized her quickly from the Internet and her description of what she would be wearing. Lena wore a mint short-sleeved suit and had a dark brown bob. Kascey and Grady extended their hands to shake hers when they met. Her smile was wide and she was a rather expressive and petite person. She picked up her briefcase as they moved to a more private location on the veranda of the restaurant.

Grady ordered beverages and snacks, and Kascey concentrated on Lena's iPad with the lists and plans for the following day.

"We have your license. Now, you have the rehearsal dinner tonight at the Flying Blue Marlin on the ground floor. It is beautiful. You will get a wonderful view of the harbor, and we have six tables booked for sixty people. Tomorrow afternoon is the big day, and we have the cars coming at two thirty to transport you from the hotel to the beach and the venue. It is only at the tip of the resort. Pastor Nottage will officiate the ceremony on the beach, and then you all will be transported back to the hotel for the reception which starts at three forty-five.

Kascey listened intently as Lena explained the process and went over the menus.

Grady was interested as the meals were described in detail. He had savored most of it before, and was looking forward to the conch dish and had ordered some fritters for the table.

"This is so splendid, and I am so excited. It is all working out as planned. I really hope that my guests will get here soon. They should have touched down by now," she said slightly anxiously.

"Do not worry. It will all happen on time. They will get here. I can check on the flight for you. Just relax and it will all fall into place," Lena was assured that it would because she had meticulous plans. "So what dress did you decide on for the dinner tonight? I know that you are a well-known designer so it must be something spectacular."

"You should see it," Kascey said laughing. "From the first time I tried it on, I knew it was the one."

Grady laughed at her explanation as he chucked down some fritters and the drink to follow. The sun was still out and he gazed out at the water. The world seemed so tranquil to him. He was calm and ready for the weekend's events.

Kascey looked toward the reception area and could see Nathalie's silhouette.

Nathalie, Trudy, Lucinda, and her parents walked through the lobby. Her mother sauntered in with a bag and Nate was followed by a bellman. They already seemed so relaxed to her.

"Grady, look some are here! There is Luce, and I see my parents." Kascey pointed toward the lobby while Grady excused himself and got up to greet them while she wrapped things up with Lena. "Come and meet our family and friends," she said.

"Thank you. That would be wonderful," she replied as Lena gathered her belongings and Grady signed the bill.

Within a minute, Kascey and Grady met the crew near the reception counter as they checked in.

Mabel hugged Kascey, and Lucinda greeted Grady.

"I was beginning to worry!" Kascey said.

"Oh no. It all went so well. And we saw some of the group at the airport. We took the bus together. Your father and I cannot wait to get to the beach and take a walk through the hotel before dinner," explained Mabel.

"Oh, please meet the planner. "This is Lena. Without her, none of this would have been possible."

"I am very pleased to meet you and thank you very much. Kascey has gone on so much about you, and we are so grateful to you for sorting this out," expressed Mabel.

"Well, the pleasure is all mine. It was so nice to work with Kascey and I hope that you will have an enjoyable stay. I have to run now to get some more things finalized. I will see you all this evening. It was lovely meeting you," Lena ensured her as she started to pace toward the entrance and grabbing her phone at the same time.

"Thanks so much. See you later," replied Kascey who remained in the reception area.

"Hello, Kascey," greeted Ethan as he walked over with the keys. He had been checking in and missed Lena.

"Hello," she responded. "I am so happy to see you all. I am so excited. Finally, the wedding is tomorrow."

"Yes, and we are delighted to be here." Ethan replied as he shook Grady's hand.

"Kascey, how are you?" Lucinda asked as she walked over with her keys.

"Fabulous. It's tomorrow and are you ready?"

"Sure. I am ready. Are *you* ready?" Lucinda replied.

"Sure I am. There is so much to look forward to. How was your flight?" She asked.

"Fabulous. We took the direct flight from JFK, and it went perfectly. I cannot wait to get to the beach before the dinner," she said.

"That is a good plan. I might join you actually, not after dark though. Grady, we should come back down after we have met everyone. Your parents should be coming soon, right?"

"Yes. They should be here any minute and we should definitely come back down," he agreed. He was open minded and could not wait to get the celebrations started. He was also waiting for the arrival of Caleb, his aunt, cousin and Claude. While Kascey awaited the arrival of Moda, Mari and Vasquez who was travelling with Daphne on his private jet.

"Fabulous. Okay, everyone we will see you in an hour or so. I am just going to wait for the others to get here while you freshen up upstairs," she informed them.

"Okay, Kascey. We will see you soon," replied Mabel. They followed the bellman upstairs as they waved to everyone.

Nathalie stayed behind a few moments to chat some more with Kascey who was still holding up at this point. They sat in the lobby with Grady and went over the times and the plans for the evening. They agreed to have an easy night, and the real festivity would begin the following day.

"We do not want you ruining that perfect glow for your wedding day now, do we?" Nathalie advised.

Grady ordered a few drinks from the bar, and they sipped and listened to the steel band play holiday tunes. More guests poured in—and so did Damien along with Kelly, Mavey, and Jane. Grady noticed his family members in an instant as well as Claude's authoritative walk and Caleb's confident stride to the counter. His godmother Sylva was also due to arrive as was Nancy, his travel writing cousin from Ireland.

Vasquez and Daphne arrived in a white stretch limo and of course he was sought after as soon as he disembarked with bellmen following behind. Tourists were snapping photos on their iPhones. He was staying in an executive suite not far from the honeymoon suite.

Ecstatically, Kascey and Grady greeted the new arrivals one by one. She was so pleased that Vasquez could make it. It was as if he had forgiven her for leaving and it was going to be a weekend of moving on. He looked so dapper as he waltzed in. Daphne was dressed for an afternoon on the coast of Saint-Tropez.

"I am so happy to see you two!" exclaimed Kascey as she greeted Vasquez and Daphne with a hug.

"We are happy to be here," replied Vasquez with the same candor that he always had. "I would not have missed it, Kascey—not for anything," he responded hugging her.

"We are so happy to be here and to celebrate this milestone with you," Daphne said in her nurturing way. "Congratulations, Kascey. We are very proud of you."

"Thank you. It makes me feel so much better that we can all move on and just have a lovely time," she expressed.

"Yes. It is time to move on and look forward to the new," replied Vasquez to which Kascey was very relieved.

They went to the counter to check in while Grady continued to chat to the guests.

"So what time is dinner again, Kascey?" Daphne politely asked as she turned to proceed to the suite.

"Half past seven, and it is going to be fabulous. You should really enjoy it," replied Kascey.

Vasquez followed confidently behind the porter, and was eager to settle in for the afternoon. "See you later, Kascey," he exclaimed as they whisked by with the luggage to the elevators. He was so noticeable in his cream linen outfit, and hotel security was now following him through the lobby.

Kascey walked toward Grady who was chatting with Kelly and Damien about the arrangements for the following day.

"At two thirty, assemble in the lobby where the staff will direct you to the coach. I should also be down at that time and if you have any more questions, we can talk further at dinner," he informed them.

"Okay, son. We are looking forward to it. We hear that the weather should be beautiful tomorrow," remarked Damien. His parents were also weary from the flight and wanted to relax before the dinner.

"Sure. We will see you at seven thirty here in the lobby," promised Kelly as they walked to the elevators.

Kascey chatted with Moda, Mari, and Nathalie on the sofas in the lobby. Moda had such elegance as she perched on the chair and made exaggerated expressions as they laughed and chatted about the flight and the evening dinner.

Claude, Caleb and Grady joined them as they went over the final plans. It was meant to be a simple march from the veranda to the open beach and Kascey had chosen her favorite classic tune for the march.

They were expecting Remy to arrive at any minute. He would take photos for the wedding in his professional New York style. Moda was looking forward to being snapped in the romantic setting by her husband.

After meeting everyone, Kascey prepared for the dinner. She looked in the mirror at her black cocktail dress, which fit perfectly. She realized that tomorrow her life would be different. She heard a knock on the door and heard her mother's voice. She rushed to open the door. "Mum? I am so happy it is you."

"Hi, dear. I had to come in to just say how proud we are of you. The atmosphere is perfect here, and I hope it all goes well for you tomorrow. I cannot wait to see you happily walking down the aisle with your father—and to have Grady waiting on the beach, it is so romantic."

"I know. It is like a fairy tale. The planner is excellent, and I really do not have to do any more because it is all arranged. I just want to thank you and Dad as well. Our honeymoon is after the holiday, and then we will go back to our lives in New York. Now, we have found a place and will start the rest of our lives together."

"It sounds wonderful, and you look as gorgeous as usual. Is that one of your designs?" She asked always flattering her.

"Yes, actually. I thought that it would be perfect for this evening. Also, the actual gown is in the closet. You can have a peek."

"Fabulous." Mabel rushed to the closet and threw open the doors. The dress was satin, sleeveless, and slim fitting. It was so bright that it almost glowed. Fine needlework contoured the edges, and it was gathered at the waist. "Beautiful. It is absolutely beautiful. Where did you find it?"

"It was specially designed by Vasquez. He says that it is his gift to me. I think that it is so gorgeous, and Grady will love it," she confided teary eyed. It was a rather remarkable dress and it was obvious that it would be admired and would make headlines.

"Oh. It is almost seven thirty. We had better join the others downstairs for the dinner," suggested Kascey.

Mabel looked at her and said, "Yes. I suppose we should. However, remember how lucky that you are—and all will be fine tomorrow." Those were Mabel's parting words to her daughter. She thought that it all went well even though she was overcome with emotion.

She and Kascey swept through the corridor and down to the lobby where the guests had assembled. As Kascey walked with each step, her past life slipped away. She took steps toward her new life.

Grady was fidgeting at the entrance to the restaurant. He hugged her and turned to go inside to be seated. The guests were seated and the decorations were marvelous. There were gold ribbons dangling from the ceiling, candles and each table was dressed in white linen tablecloths. There was a sense of mysticism as she took her seat next to Grady and the bridal party.

They ate lobster béarnaise for the main course followed by pineapple and white chocolate mousse tarts, and holiday pudding with brandy butter. There were clanking of glasses as the members rose to give many speeches. Vasquez was the first to rise to congratulate the happy couple on their upcoming nuptials.

Damien followed and welcomed his wonderful soon-to-be daughter-in-law to the family, and then Ethan welcomed Grady to his family.

Following which Caleb and Moda rose to give their speeches regarding the happy couple. Caleb had known Grady for years and decided to take the high road in his speech, and Moda was able to speak of their enduring friendship and professional escapades. The sparkling drinks poured and the band played on as the group danced the night away to jazz and calypso.

Kascey's feet were sore, and she held her heels over her shoulder as she kissed her fiancé good night after midnight. She then followed the remainder of the guests to their respective suites.

"I'll see you at the altar tomorrow," she reminded him teasingly as she shut her door and sank in the bed of the soon-to-be wedding suite.

Grady nodded in agreement and complied as he thought of their future together. It was important to get a good night's sleep to say his lines as he meant them to be said.

Chapter 22

THE BIG DAY

Kascey arose bright eyed to a festive brunch. The sliding doors of her suite opened onto a lavish patio and a wide ocean view. She thought of calling Grady, but she decided not to at the time. The ladies would arrive soon to get ready for the big day.

Mabel and Ethan decided to have breakfast downstairs and to do a bit of shopping in the resort's center. It was a sunny day and she covered her head with a wide brimmed and white straw hat. She was thrilled with excitement for a day she had waited for all of her life.

Moda, Nathalie, and Lucinda were her bridesmaids, and the groomsmen included Claude, Caleb, and cousin Max. The bridesmaids wore shimmery champagne slinky apparel, and the men were dressed in tuxedos.

By two o'clock, Kascey's suite was filled with the ladies all preparing her in some shape or form. The photographer took photos while the stylists applied finishing touches to her face. Her hair had been swept up and covered with a white satin beanie which had a tiny netted veil that only covered down to her nose so that the rest of her face was exposed. The group gathered for a last-minute photo, picked up their bouquets of white roses and silver holly, and headed for the door.

"Nervous?" asked Moda as she held the suite door open for Kascey.

"Yes, a little, but I am more excited I guess," she replied wispy and still unable to talk.

"What is the matter?" asked Nathalie concerned.

"Not much—just a few jitters. Can we check if the groomsmen have left the building?" She asked.

"Sure, we can check that," Lucinda responded as she grabbed her phone to call Nate. "Nate, hi. I am just checking to see if the coast is clear in the lobby?"

"Yes, we are all on the beach. Kelly is wondering how you are doing?" He responded surprised to hear from her.

"Thanks. Just let her know that we are all ready and are about to get in the limo."

Lucinda hung up. "All right. The coast is clear. Now that is a relief so let's get downstairs. They are all waiting for us on the beach!" She exclaimed.

"Thanks, Luce. I am so relieved about that," responded Kascey unable to elaborate and jittery. The ladies held her short train as they entered the elevator and descended to the lobby.

Lena was waiting at the entrance and motioned for them to proceed to where the driver was waiting. Elegantly, Kascey entered the limo as she heard the applause from the guests.

Guests in the lobby took photos of the bridal party leaving.

"Thank you for waiting, Lena," Kascey stated. "We were just a few minutes late, but I was worried."

"That's okay. It is to be expected. You look like a blushing bride. The dress is really beautiful. I can tell that it is a Vasquez original," marveled Lena.

"Thank you so much—and also for getting it all together. We are almost there," Kascey calculated.

The limousine drove closer to the ceremony and stopped close to the carpet that had been laid out for the party to walk. The car pulled up, and the doors slammed while the entourage exited. The photographers, including Remy, started snapping. Moda tried not to outshine the bride who was a touch of elegance in her own right.

Kascey disembarked from the car as Grady glanced back. He was in awe of her beauty, elegance, and sophistication. Kascey grabbed Ethan's arm and steadied herself on the carpet. She peered on admiringly at her future husband and smiled at the guests. The crowd gasped at her appearance.

The December sun cast a dull glow, and a slight winter sea breeze swept across the area.

Kascey looked at Grady. His eyes pierced hers, and it seemed as though there were only two people left. The crowd was silent as the march played, and she and Ethan stopped at the altar, which was decorated with roses and bougainvillea.

Grady walked closer, and Ethan extended his arm to Grady to receive the bride. "Thank you," he acknowledged with a nod and looked in her eyes again.

The pastor blushed as even he felt as if he was interfering before commencing.

He commenced and spoke clearly as the washing of the waves could be heard. There was still an ample breeze and Mabel held her shawl and a handkerchief since she could not last the ceremony without a tear. She motioned to her husband as he sat, as if to say *good job*. She had hoped to catch Kascey's glance, but there was too much to take in.

Kascey felt surreal as she grasped his firm hand and looked intently. He responded and moved in closer while the pastor raised his hand a bit as if to say not yet.

"You look gorgeous," he confided as he held her hands tighter.

"Thank you," she whispered and smiled.

The pastor continued and read the traditional marriage passage as the couple replied in customary fashion. "You may kiss the bride," he declared in a posh pronounced accent while the guests clapped and cheered. The bridal party huddled around them as he lifted Kascey off her feet and they embraced with a long kiss. She landed firmly on her feet again and smiled as they hugged and the pastor completed the ceremony.

Their family members gathered near the altar to congratulate and to hug them.

"Congratulations and best wishes, dear," Kascey heard her mother say as she hugged her.

"Thank you, Mom," she heard herself say as if in a dream.

"You look fabulous, just fabulous," she replied quickly as she moved on for another person to take her space and give their best wishes.

Grady's parents were all around him. Mavey and Jane also wished the happy couple congratulations.

Kelly officially accepted Kascey into the family. "Best wishes, Kascey. That dress looks amazing. Welcome to the Chisholm family, dear," she said as she hugged her.

"Thank you. I would not have had it any other way," she responded confidently and proudly. Vasquez and Daphne also neared the altar and congratulated the couple.

Vasquez was overcome with emotion from the ceremony as he congratulated them. He then said to Kascey, "You look exceptional. The dress has really done it for you," he observed proudly.

Vasquez from the onset had admired the dress. It was as if none of the past year had occurred and they continued where they had left in a good place. The festivities were soon to begin and a feast had been prepared at the resort.

Drinks were served at the reception for the guest as Kascey and the bridal party took photos on the sand. Kascey was mindful not to ruin the dress with the impending waves as the afternoon wore on and the tide began to rise. Grady would hold her train as they walked close to the water's edge for the opportune photo.

Their parents looked on admiringly from the deck and waited until the coach arrived to return them to the reception. The bridal party sipped more champagne on the beach and had one last group photo before heading to the cars.

The happy couple took one last photo as she turned to her husband and Lena went ahead to prepare for the reception.

Kascey said sincerely, "I love you, Grady. Thank you for being the one."

"I love you too. Thank you for making my dream come true," he replied knowing that one day they would look back and wonder where had all the time gone? From that response followed a close embrace which initiated a beginning for them.

The limousine brought the newlywed couple and the bridal party to the reception.

Kascey felt like keeping her husband to herself as a new found joy and excitement had overcome her. She realized that her guests came first and were to be catered to after having made the journey to the wedding.

When they moved through the lobby to the reception, the hotel guests applauded all around them and when she was introduced as Mrs. Grady Chisholm. The wedding party's table faced the rest of the party, and everyone looked forward to the speeches, feast, and dancing. The band had started to play as their love was shared and celebrated throughout the room.

Caleb and Moda prepared to give their speeches while the appetizers were being served. Kascey had chosen the seafood followed by more seafood and a chocolate and raspberry wedding cake.

The wedding became abuzz on social media, especially for her dress custom made by Vasquez and Moda's presence as they were spotted in the lobby of the resort. Grady was still in awe at what had occurred on the beach. The memories of which were etched in his mind like a movie scene where he played the main part. He looked over at his new bride—confident and beautiful—and felt a sense of pride. It could not have been anyone else. Kascey turned to him and raised her glass as another speech was made. He lifted his and met her eyes in acknowledgment before standing and asking for the first dance.

The guests applauded as they danced. Grady was in a dream, and they were the only ones there. Kelly and Damien and Moda and Remy followed them to the dance floor. The floor was crowded as Nate and Luce joined them, and then Ethan and Mabel. Vasquez decided to sit it out and chat with Daphne while the main course was being served.

It grew late and many guests had early flights, but the crowd remained at the reception for a while to celebrate. The dining room was beautifully and festively decorated and bursting with energy. Lena was pleased by the way it had turned out and had another wedding the following day.

"Why don't we have an early night?" Grady asked in the middle of the stanza.

"Sounds like a good plan. Our flight is early in the morning, and there is work on Monday," replied Kascey.

"Yes. I think so." Grady did have busy week as it was really the last work week of the year before they left for their real honeymoon after the holiday break. They continued to enjoy the remainder of the reception having the memories to last their whole lives.

The crowd could be heard laughing and talking while Grady and Kascey made their acknowledgments before their exit. Ethan and Mabel hugged and wished them good-bye as she would not be seeing them before the honeymoon.

Kascey said, "Happy holidays, Mom and Dad. I love you!"

"We love you too, dear. Good luck, happy holidays, and congratulations!" Mabel replied proudly as she looked into her eyes.

Lucinda had caught the bridal bouquet and felt pleased with that conquest. The younger crowd danced and ate for the remainder of the night.

It was close to midnight, and Kascey and Grady had an early morning to prepare for their flight back. They strolled from the reception hand in hand back to their suite. The rest of the season would be a blur as their euphoria would last past the season and into the new year. There was so much to look forward to. Kascey had a new business, a new marriage, and a new home with her handsome husband. He had a new wife and friend, and it seemed as if they were at the beginning and the relationship had started all over again.

Printed in the United States
By Bookmasters